Slim Down Camp

As far as Sam Zimmer is concerned, his parents might as well have sent him to prison for the summer. At Camp Thin-na-Yet the main activity is losing weight, and it's even worse than he'd imagined.

Between "active rest," "swim 'n' trim," "slimnastics," and cabin brawls, there's hardly a minute to relax. The portion-controlled meals taste worse than the foil they come wrapped in, the low-cal bug juice is so repulsive even bugs won't go near it, and there are no second helpings of anything but water. The skinny counselors confiscate hidden candy hoards and keep their own food under lock and key. And the big treat at the Saturday night dance is unlimited celery and carrot sticks.

Is there any way out? Sam can't seem to find one. Then he meets fellow sufferer Belinda Moss, and helps her stage an ill-fated raid on one of the counselors' cabins. Belinda and Sam soon agree there's only one good way to deal with the penitentiary called Camp Thin-na-Yet: escape. But that's not as easy as it sounds.

Sam's and Belinda's attempts to resolve their very real frustrations about Camp Thin-na-Yet— and about themselves—lead to a climax that's as hopeful as it is hilarious.

Slim Down Camp

Stephen Manes

Slim Down
Camp

Houghton Mifflin/Clarion Books/New York

Houghton Mifflin/Clarion Books
52 Vanderbilt Avenue, New York, NY 10017

Library of Congress Cataloging in Publication Data
Manes, Stephen.   Slim down camp.
Summary: Sent to a summer camp for overweight children,
a boy and girl rebel against the camp's authorities and
discover their own effective method of losing weight.
[1. Weight control—Fiction. 2. Camping—Fiction] I. Title.
PZ7.M31264S [Fic] 80-22725 ISBN 0-395-30170-X

Cover art by Diane Teske Harris

for Esther

1

It wasn't really *my* weight problem. It was everybody else's. Everybody kept telling me I was fat. I don't know why—I mean, I only weighed 873 pounds.

Anyway, that's how people made me feel sometimes. Actually I was 164, exactly twenty-four pounds above my ideal weight. Chubby, maybe. Pudgy. Plump. But not really fat.

I know, I know, that's what every fat person says. And those ideal weight charts are for people with clothes on, but I had to fiddle with the dial on the scale and make it read a little under zero and then jump on stark naked to make it come out right. So actually I was maybe twenty-eight pounds overweight. Say thirty. I didn't think that was so terrible. But other people kept making a big deal about it.

Especially my parents, who aren't exactly stringbeans themselves. What they are is terrific cooks. It's sort of their hobby. And it's not easy to be thin when you get fed things like roast suckling pig and chicken paprikash and fettucine Alfredo and lobster Thermidor and chocolate mousse pie and Italian cheesecake. Not to mention homemade cake and cookie and candy snacks.

1

Oh, sometimes they'd decide it was time to go on a diet, but those diets usually lasted about a week. My strategy for those periods was a heavy dose of dietary supplements such as Hershey bars and Necco wafers and Ding Dongs, which are available in drugstores without a prescription. Just because your parents raise you on gourmet food doesn't mean you lose your appetite for junk.

Anyway, eggs Benedict was what we were eating for breakfast one wintry Sunday morning while we read *The New York Times*. "Listen to this," my Mom said, wiping a dab of Hollandaise sauce from her chin. "'Slim Down at Camp Bellefonte. Re-education in nutrition, wide variety of exercise and activity in a medically supervised program. 956 pounds lost last summer.' There must be a dozen of these reducing camps."

"Are you planning to enroll?" I asked with my mouth full.

Mom gave me one of her patented looks. "Frankly, Sam, I had it in mind for you."

"Sounds like Camp Siberia to me. They probably clamp your mouth shut so you can't eat."

"That might be better than what happened two summers ago." She was referring to the fact that I'd come home from camp fifteen pounds heavier than when I'd left, which had always bothered her a lot more than it did me. "Maybe we should look into this, Irv."

"Okay with me," Dad said, reaching for the homemade grapefruit marmalade.

"Not with me," I said. I'd had enough of camp two years ago. The ad had shown happy campers enjoying every possible activity (except the one nobody talks about in front of kids) and learning useful skills. Actually you got to do each activity precisely once, except for the ones you didn't like. And the only skill you got to practice was tolerating obnoxious people.

Last year I'd talked my way out of camp by going on about how much I wanted to study for a ham radio license, after which I loafed around all summer and kind of gave up on ham radio. But this year Mom and Dad were planning to attend a convention in Stockholm in August, so they were determined to get me out of the house for a while. They're both systems analysts, and according to their analysis, a "Slim Down Camp" would be the perfect thing for my system.

I didn't agree. For one thing, I really wanted to study some journalism books so I'd have a chance at making the high-school paper in the fall. And after a hard year at school, I wanted to relax. There was just no way I was going to spend my summer vacation counting calories.

I was firm about it. I refused. I yelled. I screamed. I threatened to drown myself in the Delaware River. And in the middle of July, I found myself in New Hampshire, heading for a place called "Camp Thin-na-Yet".

2

A mile and six-tenths down the rockiest road in the entire universe, there it was, shimmering in the heat: a gravel parking lot full of cars, a big mess hall with a couple of metallic-green flies buzzing around the garbage bins, and a wide brown lawn with a flagpole at one end and a couple of dozen groups of kids and parents and counselors standing all over it.

"We're late," Mom said. "I told you we should've gotten an earlier start, Irv."

Dad shrugged and glanced in my direction. "Some people had to have thirds on their hotcakes."

"You're in the red group," Mom informed me. As if I didn't know; she'd only bought eighty rolls of red tape to mark my stuff with. As we got out of the hot car, she stared at the signposts on the lawn. "Pink, yellow, purple . . . I don't see a red sign."

That was because she was looking toward the girls' groups. Also because somebody had turned the red sign around so you couldn't see it from where we were. But you could hardly miss the pile of red-tagged sleeping bags up ahead. I jogged up and tossed mine onto the heap.

"Hey, another red!" somebody shouted.

4

"Is this the red group?" my mother asked a tall, skinny guy in a Camp Thin-na-Yet T-shirt. His "Counselor" nametag said "Maury."

"No, we're the pink and purple polka dots," said a big roly-poly kid with a New York accent, apple cheeks, and breath that smelled like the city dump. Not that most of the kids weren't roly-poly. Looking around, I almost felt thin.

"Let's not be snotty till lunchtime, okay, Julius?" Maury said.

"*I'm* Julius," said a kid who looked like the Michelin Man only flabby.

"Then who are *you?*" Maury pointed to the kid with the New York accent.

"Brutus," he said, putting his hand on his nametag so the counselor couldn't read it.

"I give up," Maury sighed, sticking his bony hand toward my parents. Man, was he thin! I felt enormous again just looking at him. Amidst a sea of big round curves, this guy was all knees and elbows and ankles, like those long-distance runners you see in marathons. "I'm Maury Bowen. This is the red cabin."

"Irv and Lynn Zimmer," my Dad said. "That's Sam."

"Pleased to meet you," Maury told my parents, and checked me off on his clipboard. "I think your son will really have an excellent learning experience up here." He said this in a tone that implied my father should start thinking about how much of a tip he'd come up with at the end of the summer.

5

"Can we take a look around?" Dad asked.

"Sure," Maury said. "Why don't you join that group of parents over there? Somebody'll be along in a minute or two to give you a tour."

"See you later," Dad told me, and he and Mom walked off.

"You're not fat," said the kid who called himself "Brutus," but whose nametag read "Nick Barris."

"That's what I keep telling everybody," I replied.

" 'Slimmer' Zimmer," Nick said. "That's what we ought to call you." Just what I needed: a "Nick" name.

"That makes everybody," Maury announced. "What say we head down to the cabin?"

"What say we head to lunch?" said Nick Barris. Everybody laughed.

We all picked up our sleeping bags and started down the path. The place was really woodsy. You could hear all kinds of chirping and croaking and buzzing and clacking in the air. A little transparent bug landed on my arm, and I squashed it with my free hand. It burst in a little pool of blood. Mine.

"You have to *flick* those off," a sad-looking kid with thick black-rimmed glasses advised me. "Otherwise, their stinger goes right into you."

"You sound like an expert," I said, checking his nametag, which said "Franklin Delano Schwartz."

"Sort of." He shrugged. "I was up here last year."

"How'd you like it?" I asked.

"I lost thirty pounds."

"Why are you back?"

6

He grinned. "I put forty on again."

Up ahead, a kid named Howard Andeker was trying to strike up a conversation with Maury. Andeker had a bored, superior air, as though he had better things to do than associate with us children. "What are you studying in college?" he asked Maury.

"Sociology."

"What's that?" whined a short redheaded kid whose nametag said "Russell Duff."

"The study of what people do in groups," Andeker informed him.

"Hey, you're studying us, then?" Nick asked Maury.

"You never know," Maury said slyly. "Better be on your best behavior."

"Hey, look!" shouted a stubby dark-haired kid with a face rounder than Charlie Brown's and a belly to match. He stooped down for a second. A little brown toad jumped in the air. "Boy, that's neat," said the kid, whose name seemed to be Bernie Androsky. "Maybe I'll end up liking this camp after all."

"I wouldn't count on it," Franklin Delano Schwartz mumbled to himself.

Despite all the shade, the heat was getting worse. What I could've used right then was a nice big air conditioner and a quart of orange soda. Fat chance.

"Left turn," Maury shouted, and we walked up a little path to a cabin with a bright red door. "Okay, guys, this is it. Leave your bags on the porch."

The inside of the cabin wasn't a whole lot bigger than my bedroom at home; the difference was that it

7

was supposed to serve for seven of us. The way they crammed us all in was by using bunk beds, which looked like war surplus. Revolutionary War. I had the vision of being in a lower berth and having one of these huge guys fall on me while I was sleeping. I could just see the headline: CAMPER CRUSHED BY FALLING FLAB. I decided I'd get myself an upper berth no matter what.

The wooden floor made a lot of noise, so everybody started tramping hard to see just how loud it could get. I hoped the floor was strong enough to take it. "Quiet down," Maury shouted over the din. "You'll find your footlockers beside the beds, two apiece, and that's how we'll assign partners for now. If you want to trade around later, fine, but right now just arrange things with whoever's assigned to you. If you can't agree on who gets the upper and who gets the lower, flip for it."

Big commotion. I found my trunk. "Where's House?" I yelled. That was the name on the trunk beside mine.

"That's me," shouted Julius from the other end of the room.

"You said it," Nick laughed. "Wide as one."

"Not very original, bare-ass," said Julius. He came over and stood beside me. "How about if I have the bottom?" he asked. "Too much trouble to keep climbing up all the time."

"Fine with me." I swung myself up to see how it felt on top. A little shaky, actually, but if I fell through in the middle of the night, I'd have a nice soft spot to land on. And from up top, I could see everything: the cobwebs on the ceiling, the guys arguing about who'd sleep where, Maury standing at the door patiently smirking at us. And Franklin D. Schwartz, who didn't have a bunkmate, flipping a coin to decide which berth he wanted. He won the upper, but after trying it he decided the lower was probably handier after all.

"Okay, everybody out on the porch," Maury said. "Your parents are coming up."

You always hope your parents won't embarrass you in front of other kids. The potential for disaster's always there. You never know when your mother or father is going to say something dumb. If my parents goofed up this time, the other kids might not let me forget it for the next six weeks. So I hoped my hardest as we went inside together.

"How does the rest of the place look?" I asked.

"You ought to have some fun," Dad said.

"The toilet facilities aren't exactly pristine," Mom commented. I hoped nobody'd heard that, but Nick Barris was rolling his eyes toward the ceiling, laughing silently into his hand, and pointing at me. He didn't seem to have any parents that belonged to him.

"Where do you sleep?" Mom asked. As I was pointing out my bunk, Julius and an older man who was almost his double came through the door sideways, one at a time.

"Hi," Julius said shyly. "Dad, this is my bunkmate, Sam Zimmer."

9

Julius's dad shook my hand. "Glad to know you. Doesn't look like you have much to lose," he said, giving my stomach a pat.

"Oh, he's got some reducing to do, all right," my father said, extending his hand. "Irv Zimmer."

"Phil House. Looks like these boys are in for quite a summer."

"Is Mrs. House here?" my Mom asked.

"I'm a widower," Mr. House said.

"Oh," Mom said. "I'm sorry."

"We get along," said Mr. House. "Don't we, Julius?"

Julius nodded.

"My boy here's the best cook in the state of Ohio," his father said proudly. "Of course, I hope he'll develop some other interests here in camp."

"I'm sure he will," Mom said. "What sorts of things do you cook, Julius?"

Mom is always on the lookout for new recipes, but before Julius had a chance to answer her, a bugle blew some dumb tune outside. No: it was a record of a bugle coming from a P.A. system. You could tell it was a record because of all the scratches you heard.

"Okay, parents," Maury said. "Visiting hours are just about over. We'd appreciate it if you said your goodbyes outside."

We went out. My mother was telling me to be sure and brush my teeth and not to get sunburned and stuff like that, so I tuned her out for a while and tuned in Franklin Schwartz's father, who was telling his son not to eat too much and to try to get along with the other kids better this year, and then I heard Russell Duff's mom say something about taking his allergy pills, and then my Mom asked me if I was listening, and I said of course, and she told me to cut my toenails when they got too long, and then Dad interrupted her and told me the important thing was to have a good time. And maybe lose a few pounds. Then the scratchy bugle tooted again, and Maury said it was time to leave, and mom kissed me and said to take care, and Dad shook my hand and said to have fun, and then they joined the other parents and started up the path.

It felt weird to watch them disappear. Even though I'd been to camp before, it still gave me this strange, creepy feeling like a prisoner or an orphan or somebody. It's hard to describe: in a way it felt good to get away from home and my parents, sort of like the first day of school after a long summer vacation. But at least in school you've heard something from the older kids about what your teachers and your classes will be like, and you always go home at the end of the day. Up here I was stuck for the next six weeks with whatever got thrown my way. And what that might be—well, as my history teacher was fond of saying every six minutes, "God only knows. And he ain't tellin'."

So I was feeling kind of lumpy in the throat when Nick Barris's voice broke the gloom. "When do we eat?" he yelled.

3

Back in the cabin, Maury put on a serious face. "Okay, we're on our own now. It's up to us. Nobody's going to come in and pick up after us, nobody's going to sweep the floor for us, and we're the ones who decide how this place is going to look. So I've got a few suggestions."

It was just like the camp I went to before. "Suggestions" meant rules.

"Number one, I want you to use those drawers and hangers for your clothes. This place is too small to have everybody pulling out their trunk when they want something. And keep those drawers neat. Fold your socks and underwear, don't just stuff them in every which way. Second, I want to see those beds made in the morning before we go up to breakfast. No reason this place should look like a pigsty. And third, you all ought to write home at least every couple days. Sound fair?"

Everybody sort of half nodded. "I'm starved," Nick said.

"You really look it," said Howard Andeker. His tone was still nonchalant, but he was obviously mad about getting stuck with the upper bunk.

"That's once, you moron," Nick said, trying to sound tough.

"Oh, before I forget," Maury remembered. "Anybody got any candy, cookies—anything edible—in their footlocker?"

Seven heads shook solemnly.

"You sure, now?"

Seven heads nodded.

" 'Cause if I find anything, not only do I have to confiscate it, but you have to go without your next meal. Everybody clear on that?"

More nodding.

"Okay, then. Let's get some lunch."

The magic word! Six of us shoved our way to the door. Franklin Schwartz didn't seem to be in any hurry. "You're not hungry?" I asked as I pushed past him.

"I had a big breakfast," he said in that forlorn way of his. So had I, but it hadn't spoiled my appetite.

"Where you from?" Nick asked me as we started up the hill.

"Cherry Hill, New Jersey," I said.

"Sounds like a dump."

"It's a suburb of Philadelphia."

"That's even worse, Slimmer. A suburb of a dump. Anybody here from a real city?"

"Cleveland," Julius said.

"That's not a city, that's an armpit," Nick said.

"Where are you from?" Julius asked. "Fat City?"

"Fun City. New York, New York," Nick said proudly. "The Big Apple."

"The big asshole, you mean," Julius said. Everybody laughed.

"Hey, any of you been there?" Nick demanded.

"Me," I said, along with everybody else but Howard Andeker, who probably had been, but was too busy acting bored to admit it.

"Well, then you all know how great New York is. I don't have to say another word," Nick said.

"Excellent idea," said Howard Andeker.

"Where *you* from, hotshot?" Nick asked.

Andeker didn't bother to answer.

"The planet Jupiter," Nick snorted.

"Right," Andeker said. "It's a hell of a lot more likely to support human life than New York City."

Nick didn't have an answer for that one.

At the top of the hill, the parking lot was nearly empty, and the signs had disappeared from the lawn. But clusters of kids were salivating in front of the mess hall.

"God, what pigs," Nick said, looking over the crop of girls.

"They're saying exactly the same thing about you, Porky," said Howard Andeker. Nick just glared at him.

They both had a point. As far as physical attractiveness went, the only people worth looking at were the counselors. Not a fat one, not a plump one, not even one you could call chubby in the whole bunch.

14

The guys looked as though they belonged on network sports shows, and the women would've had a chance to be movie stars if they made movies in New Hampshire.

Anybody with the IQ of a turnip could've figured it out: the idea was to provide us with models of our thinner selves, so we'd imitate them. But what I wondered was why you should go to all the trouble of losing weight if all it would get you was a job herding fat kids around. Obviously you weren't supposed to look at it that way.

The P.A. system blew chow call, and we all went inside. It was the usual big hall with rows and rows of long tables and a counter with people in white uniforms at one end. At the other end, over the fireplace, where regular camps had wooden plaques listing the members of the One Match Club since the birth of Christ, we had a huge green blackboard with people's names chalked in. The names were by cabin in alphabetical order, which meant I was at the bottom, as usual: Zimmer, S.—172. As soon as I realized what that 172 meant, I suddenly got this creepy feeling.

Which got creepier when I realized what was wrong with this mess hall. It smelled funny. Not the way most mess halls smell funny, with that disgustingly yucky odor of stale mashed potatoes and lumpy gravy and overcooked cabbage—something like getting caught in the middle of all the world's cafeterias at three in the afternoon. That's the smell you expect. This room didn't smell at all. That's what was creepy.

Maury took a little red flag from a stand on the table. "Okay," he said. "One of us has to take the flag up to the counter to get our food, and somebody else has to go with him and get the drinks. Any volunteers?"

Franklin Schwartz raised his hand, and when nobody else volunteered, Howard Andeker bent his arm in the weariest way. Maury handed Frank the flag.

"Man, I could eat a moving van," Nick said.

Russ Duff nodded. "I wonder what we're having."

"I'll eat anything," said Bernie Androsky. "If there's one thing I'm not, it's fussy."

It wasn't long before our waiters returned. Howard had two big aluminum pitchers. Franklin opened a wooden box and handed Nick a sealed foil tray from it.

"Hey, what is this?" Nick demanded.

"Lunch," Frank said.

"Lunch? A flaking TV dinner?" Nick blustered. Actually, "flaking" wasn't the exact word he used.

"There are ladies present," Maury said.

"And they're getting TV dinners, too," said Nick, noticing the action at the next table. "What in hell goes on here?"

Russ Duff passed me my tinfoil slab. I ripped the cover off. What stared back at me was half an American cheese sandwich on soggy white bread, a bunch

16

of raw carrots, and some pineapple rings. I couldn't believe it. "This isn't even a TV snack," I said. "It wouldn't feed a mosquito."

"Hey, Franklin, you're the expert. Is this *it?*" Julius asked.

" 'Fraid so," Frank replied.

"Are the dinners like this, too?" asked Russell Duff in amazement.

"The dinners are hot," Frank mumbled.

"Do *you* eat this stuff?" Andeker asked Maury.

Maury nodded. "Sure do."

"Along with a lot of other crap from the counselors' mess," Frank Schwartz said matter-of-factly.

"I'll die!" Nick screamed. "I can't survive on this!"

"Look, guys," Maury said sternly. "You've got two choices: you can spend all your time grousing about the food you don't get, or you can enjoy the food you do get and spend the rest of your time enjoying something else. It's entirely up to you."

We were all too stunned to say anything. "What's in the pitchers?" Nick asked finally.

I poured some green liquid into my glass. "Bug juice."

"Low-cal bug juice," Franklin corrected me.

He was right. Regular bug juice never won any prizes, but this stuff was absolutely undrinkable. I took one taste and spit it out. "Water!" I gasped.

"Right over there," Maury said cheerfully. "Unlimited quantities, from the purest mountain springs. Best of all, not a single calorie." He pointed

17

to a rack of plastic glasses and a tap. I walked toward them.

All around me, the scene was pretty much the same. Except for repeaters like Franklin, nobody could believe this lunch. Nobody could believe this was going to be our eating pattern for the next six weeks.

For most of us, food was the only thing that kept us going. I mean, when you're fat, you don't get a whole lot of compliments. People will even make wisecracks about you to your face. But food doesn't talk back, except to make you belch or fart, and usually it makes you feel good inside. So we fatties lived and died for our meals, not to mention our desserts, our snacks, our between-snack snacks, and whatever else we could stuff into our mouths. Food was our only crutch, and this camp was kicking it out from under us.

"Damn!" muttered the kid in front of me at the water tap. "I'll kill my parents on visitors' day."

"I'll roast 'em for you," said the girl behind me. "We can have a feast."

"Be sure to invite me," I said.

"Only if you bring some fried counselor." She smiled. Her gray eyes were really kind of pretty. Eyes don't get fat.

I smiled back, but I couldn't think of anything else to say, so I filled two water glasses and carted them back to the table. "One way to make your food seem like more," Maury was lecturing, "is to chew it slower. Make it last." This useful information started a slow-chewing contest. Everybody was chomping so exaggeratedly that a cow would've come in last.

"You win the disgustingness award, Barris," said Andeker, peeved that Nick insisted on opening his mouth between each chew. Nick's reply was to stick out his tongueful of half-eaten carrots.

"Leave it hanging there, Barris," Andeker said. "Maybe I'll pull it off."

Nick swallowed. "Take a long walk off a short pier."

"Original," Andeker sneered. "You masticator."

Nick turned red. "Take that back!" Andeker just laughed.

"Hey, is he allowed to call me that?" Nick asked Maury.

"It's a free country," Maury said.

"Calm down, Barris," said Frank Schwartz. "A masticator is somebody who chews."

Nick looked surprised. "Yeah. I know that." Sure he did.

I noticed another weird thing about this mess hall. Not only didn't it have the mess-hall smell, but it also didn't have the mess-hall sound of clattering plates. When we were done eating, we just stacked our aluminum trays and plastic cups in the middle of the table. They made a sort of squeaky sound.

"If you're into ecology," Maury said, "you'll be happy to know we recycle all those trays."

"If you're into ecology," Andeker said disgustedly,

19

"you'll be happy to know you can wash good old china dishes and use them over again."

Maury ignored him. "You two," he said, pointing to me and Julius, "bus the stuff." We dumped the pitchers into a gray plastic bin beside the food counter, tossed the trays into a can marked "foil," and crammed everything else into the trash.

"This place eats it," Julius said.

"What you mean is, we don't," I said.

He gave me a sly grin. "We'll see," he whispered.

At the end of the room where the blackboards were, a bald, bearded guy in a Camp Thin-na-Yet T-shirt climbed up on a little stage and tapped a microphone. It screeched like fingernails on a balloon. "Can you all hear me?" he asked.

"No!" a lot of us shouted back.

He ignored it. "I'm Dr. Langer, the camp director." Nobody applauded. In fact, Nick and some guy on the other side of the room booed. Langer paid no attention. "I want to welcome you all to Camp Thin-na-Yet. I hope you'll all have a really enjoyable summer."

"How, when we're starving?" someone shouted. Everybody laughed. A bunch of us yelled, "Yeah!"

Dr. Langer waved his hands in the air. "All right, simmer down. Obviously, most of you are accustomed to eating more for lunch than you had today. But you're all up here to lose weight, and you're not going to do it with some magical operation or some miracle drug."

"I'm not going to do it, period," Julius mumbled.

"You're going to do it by changing the bad habits you've fallen into," Langer went on. "Now, a few of you have been here before, and you know how things work, so you'll have to bear with us while we explain it to the rest. Okay, you all see the chart up there behind me. Your starting weight's up there now, but that won't count. Beginning tomorrow, you'll weigh yourselves every morning before breakfast, and we'll post your current weight up there at lunchtime alongside your weight at the beginning of the week.

"Each week, you'll have a weight-loss goal. If you meet the goal, you'll get a special privilege. Sometimes we even have bonus privileges for those of you who do an extra-good job. But if you start gaining weight, or if you fall back after you start losing, it isn't going to be much fun for you. So what I suggest you do, every one of you, is *get your attitude geared up toward taking off those pounds!* Your counselors are here to help you do it. You can rely on them for advice. I'm here to help with special problems, and I'll meet you all individually within the next few days.

"That does it for now. Have fun."

He stepped down from the stage, and one of the woman counselors stepped up. She looked more like a movie star than any of the others, probably because she was wearing about half a ton of makeup and a Camp Thin-na-Yet T-shirt that stretched so tight across her chest you could barely read it. When she went to the mike, even some of the nine-year-olds were whistling and drooling and shouting, but she smiled us all down with this crushingly superior look that reminded me of the way some mothers treat their five-year-olds.

"Now we'll find out if there's any singing talent this year," she said with a gummy smile. "I'm going to teach you the words to our camp song."

This sounds so dumb I'm ashamed to even write it down, but here is what she sang:

> We're gonna make new friends
> At Camp Thin-na-Yet.
> We're gonna make new friends
> At Camp Thin-na-Yet.
> We're gonna make new friends,
> We're gonna start new trends,
> We're gonna slim down our rear ends
> At Camp Thin-na-Yet.

She even wiggled her butt when she came to the part about "rear ends." Then she commanded us to sing along.

It embarrassed me. It actually gave me goose pimples. What we should've done was yell "No way!" But except for one or two voices who made snide remarks and clammed up, most of us mumbled the words.

"You can do better than that," said Miss Shirt,

which was what Nick called her. "Everybody sing!" And we did. Somehow she had us in her grasp. "One more time! Let's really hear it now!" And damned if we didn't sing out loud and clear. I felt like two cents. Make that one cent. A piece of bubble gum. Already chewed.

We sang a bunch of other songs, the old ones people only sing at camp, like "Bingo" and "There Were Three Jolly Fishermen," and a lot more so memorable I forget them, and then it was time for another rousing chorus of the camp theme. Miss Shirt told us what excellent singers we were, and at long last, lunch hour was over.

"When do we eat?" Nick Barris asked. Nobody bothered to laugh.

4

"I'll just have that watermelon," Julius told the scrawny canteen girl.

"Name?"

"Barris. Nick Barris."

The girl checked off "Barris" on her clipboard and handed Julius a sliver of watermelon on a paper plate. "No, no. I want *that* watermelon!" He pointed to a whole one behind her.

"You're holding up the line," she said, with a look of contempt only thin people know how to give. "Next!"

"Hell!" Julius muttered. He picked up his plate and stalked off.

We had a choice of fruit or sugarless gum, and I was damned if I was going to pick anything wrapped in foil. I got a slice of cantaloupe so thin you could read a newspaper through it. Almost a whole mouthful.

"Fruits have hardly any calories," Maury was explaining, "so they're terrific desserts when you're trying to lose weight."

"How would you know?" Russell Duff whined.

"How much do you think I weigh now?" Maury asked.

"Six twenty-two," Julius guessed.

"One fifty-four, wiseguy," Maury said. "You know how much I weighed five years ago?"

"Hey!" Nick shouted from the canteen line. "Who used my name over here?" Everybody ignored him.

"Obviously," Andeker told Maury, "you are going to tell us you lost some incredible amount, so why don't you stop the guessing game and let us in on it?"

"All right," Maury said. "One sixty-three."

"You lost nine lousy pounds?" Julius sniffed. "What'd you do, give up peanut butter cups for Lent?"

"The point is, I wanted to lose it, I lost it, and I've kept it off."

"Bravo," sneered Russ Duff.

Nick arrived with his watermelon. "You'll get yours for this, House," he said.

"I already got *my* dessert," Julius said. "What I wanted to get was *yours*." Nick just fumed.

The rest of the day didn't win any prizes. A lesson in bedmaking. A tour of the camp. A hike. Filet of minnow, mashed potato eye, and buttered green bean for dinner. A pep talk and more camp songs around the flagpole. A shoving match between Nick and Julius at the latrines. And a discussion of what would happen if you ate a whole tube of toothpaste.

After lights out, Maury told a ghost story I'd heard before. Then he left for the counselors' cabin. Once his footsteps faded out, we were alone in the dark. Crickets chirped outside. Russell Duff belched. Everybody cracked up.

Nick responded with a three-parter: a high belch,

25

a low burp, and a deep bass boomer. Androsky sang a high-low combination. I tried my famous sliding burp, but it caught in the middle and made me cough. Everybody thought that was funnier still.

"Ambulance!" Nick shouted. "Bring this man some Twinkies, quick!"

"Help! Mr. Goodbars!" Androsky groaned.

"Ding Dongs!" I yelled.

The bed shook. Julius stood up. I heard what sounded like his footlocker scraping across the floor. It was too dark to see much beside shadows, but as Frank Schwartz cried "Oreos!" I could hear Julius open the metal latches of his trunk and root around inside. He shut it again just as Andeker mumbled "Bubble Yum Gum." Then Julius plodded around the room.

I heard a faint sound of rustling paper, a very familiar sound I couldn't quite place. A couple of thank-yous. More rustling. Julius coming back to our bunk.

"Here," he mumbled, handing me something round and paper-wrapped with a stick at the bottom. Even in the dark, I knew what it was.

"This is my party, guys," he whispered loud enough for everybody to hear. "I want all the wrappers and sticks when you're done so I can destroy the evidence."

"I don't think we should do this," Frank warned.

"Say the word, and I'll take yours back," Julius offered. Schwartz didn't say a thing.

"Okay, then," Julius said. "Enjoy yourselves."

And everybody quietly began sucking on his Tootsie Roll Pop. Mine was pineapple, my favorite. I could feel my teeth decaying, but my taste buds sent up a shriek of glee.

"God, this is good," Nick moaned.

"Thank you, Mr. House," said Andeker grandly.

Then we heard it. We all heard it. Rustling in the leaves outside. It might be an animal. But the most likely animal was the one that wore a counselor's T-shirt. I couldn't see what anybody else was doing, but I stuck the wrapper back on my lollipop and slid it between the sheets. It would make you feel like the stupidest moron in the world to get caught sucking a lollipop your first night in camp. And I didn't intend to miss out on breakfast, even if it was likely to be a bowl of Kellogg's Air Flakes.

The noise came nearer, and a light came with it. I could hear paper and bedsheets flying. Then Maury tramped up the steps and came through the door carrying a lantern.

We all looked toward him. On the floor beside Bernie Androsky's bunk, I saw the worst: a Tootsie Pop wrapper. Cherry. It was so close to Bernie that he must've been the only one who couldn't see it. Above him, the look on Russell Duff's face made it obvious he was the one who'd dropped it.

"I forgot to tell you guys," Maury said, looking around the room. "I'm hanging the lantern on the hook at the bottom of the stairs. If you have to go to

27

the can, take it with you." He turned toward the Tootsie Pop wrapper.

"Just be sure to stick it back up on the hook when you come back." He was staring right past that wrapper. How could he miss it?

"Everybody squared away?"

Everybody mumbled yes.

"Good. See you in the morning." Maury walked out the door, tramped down the steps, hung up the lantern, and went to his cabin. Nick leaned out of his bed, reached out, and grabbed the wrapper.

"Nice go, Duff," he hissed. "We're lucky we're still getting breakfast tomorrow."

"It fell out when I pulled up the sheets," Duff whined.

"God, what a wimp," Nick said.

"Forget it," Julius said. "Forget it. Everybody's entitled to make a mistake."

"Not when it might cost me my breakfast, they're not," Nick grumbled.

My stomach grumbled, too. I told it help was on the way, and then I sucked myself to sleep.

5

"Food! Food!" my stomach screamed at the crack of dawn, in rhythm with the hoots and toots of some weird bird that sounded like an electronic synthesizer gone crazy. I couldn't do anything about the bird, but I figured maybe I could drown out that voice complaining beneath my navel. I climbed out of bed, went down to the latrine and gulped down as much water as I could hold. My stomach was not fooled one bit.

Back at the cabin I daydreamed about banana splits until the loudspeakers blew reveille. Then Maury bounded through the door as bright and cheerful as if he'd won a million dollars, yelling "Everybody up-up-*up!*" and shaking our beds back and forth.

Getting dressed was an ordeal. The night before, getting ready for bed, it was dark enough so you didn't get the feeling everybody in the cabin was checking out your bod. But in daylight the rolls and folds and protrusions were obvious. We were all more or less alike: rolling, sagging hulks of fatness. And more or less pearly white, with the exception of Nick. When you're fat, you generally don't go sunbathing unless you're willing to fight for your dignity.

29

We were all dressed when Maury brought in a bathroom scale and set it down in front of the door. "Okay, who wants to go first?"

"Why not?" Andeker sighed, stepping aboard.

"Two hundred thirteen," Maury said, jotting it down on his ever-present clipboard.

"That's too high," Andeker protested.

"You said it, not me."

"I don't weigh that much," Andeker insisted. "I checked before I left yesterday."

"Try again," Maury said wearily.

Howard stepped off the scale and stepped back on again. His weight came out exactly the same. "You tell me. After what I had to eat yesterday, how could I gain five pounds?"

"Maybe gravity's heavier up here," Julius joked.

"Maybe you went to a smorgasbord for a midnight-snack," Nick said.

Andeker shook his head disgustedly and got off the scale. Frank Schwartz got on. "One hundred ninety?" Maury said, surprised. "Your records from last year show one eighty-five as your top."

"Yeah, well . . ." Frank shrugged.

"I told you those scales were off," Howard said.

I stepped on. "One seventy-one," Maury reported. "A pound under what your parents told us."

"Go home," Julius said good-naturedly. "You're spoiling it for the rest of us." He stepped on.

"I hope that's a heavy-duty scale," Nick Barris cracked.

"I hope you've got a heavy-duty face," Julius shot back, " 'cause it's gonna meet up with a heavy-duty fist one of these days."

After Maury left, Frank Schwartz went around the back of the cabin and dumped half a million rocks and stones from his pockets. "What's that all about?" I asked.

"You get privileges based on the weight you lose."

I nodded.

"Well, now I can lose a quick five pounds when I need to."

"Oh," I said.

"You should've, too. You're going to have a hard time, being thin to start with." I wasn't quite sure what Frank meant, but he disappeared in the direction of the latrines before I had a chance to ask him.

At breakfast, we each got a vitamin pill. Bernie Androsky chewed his. He insisted it was the best-tasting thing he'd eaten since leaving home.

Langer's office was up by the mess hall, so we stayed in the neighborhood after breakfast. The idea was for us to keep active by playing volleyball while we waited for our individual consultations with The Boss. Of course, Maury was the only one who was any good at the game. The rest of us either screwed up trying to show off or just made feeble, half-hearted efforts. Meanwhile, Langer called us to his office one at a time in alphabetical order.

As usual, that meant I was last. When I got to Langer's office, he had his feet up on his desk. He had a cigarette in his mouth and was riffling through a folder that seemed to contain the stuff my parents and I had to fill out before I came up here. As I sat down, I noticed a diploma on one wall and a "Think Thin" sign on the other.

"So," Langer said, stretching it out like a long sigh and blowing smoke in my direction. "Sam Zimmer. Age fourteen. Special interests: journalism, comic books, baseball. 'A' student, college prep courses."

I didn't know whether I was supposed to smile or frown or yawn or what. I settled for a sort of half-shrug.

"Tell me," Langer said, pointing at me with his cigarette, "how do you feel about yourself?"

"Hungry," I said.

"What else?"

What are you supposed to say to a question like that? I'm a terrific guy? I'm okay? I settled for "I don't know."

"Well, how do you feel about your overweight problem?"

"Fat."

"Why?"

"Because I eat too much."

"Why?"

"Because I like to eat."

"Why?"

This was getting to be like a game for three-year-olds. "I have to eat to survive."

"You don't have to stuff yourself to survive. Maybe if you knew why you were overweight, you'd cut down on your eating."

"Maybe."

Langer leaned back in his chair. "All right, Sam. You want to know why you eat too much?"

I shrugged.

"Two reasons. Number one, insecurity. Unfortunately, that tends to feed on itself, so it's difficult to overcome. We concentrate on number two: habit. You are in the habit of eating, and not just when you're hungry. When you don't have anything else to do, or when you're feeling bad, or tired, or sometimes just for fun, you eat. You're programmed to eat. Am I right?"

"I guess."

"Okay. The way to get thin is to break that habit so you won't go thinking about a candy bar every time you're a little bored. When you do eat, you'll eat something that's good for you and low in calories so you'll feel full but you won't gain weight. You see my point?"

"Yeah."

"Have you noticed any examples of what I'm talking about since you've been here?"

Did he think I was an idiot? "Yeah," I said.

"Like what?"

"Like no snacks. Like the canteen giving us fruit instead of candy. Like those tiny meals which taste so lousy we can't possibly enjoy them. I get it, all right. You're trying to take the fun out of eating."

"Right! What are you going to do about it?"

What I wanted to say was, "Complain every chance I get, you jerk, and stuff myself with Julius's candy.

33

You smoke like a locomotive, which is also a lousy habit, but I don't see anybody hiding your cigarettes. If I want to lose weight, I can do it without your help."

That's what I wanted to say. What I said was, "I'll try and lose some weight." If there's one thing most adults hate, it's logic. Obedience they love.

"Attaboy," he said.

See?

"What'd he tell you?" Julius asked me as we walked down toward the cabin.

"That we're not going to get anything to eat around here," I said. "What'd he tell you?"

"That I'd like myself a lot better if I was thinner. You know what I told him? 'Maybe so, but then there'd be less of me to like.'"

"What'd he say?"

"If I got thinner, I'd like what was left of me all the more."

"Maybe he has a point."

"It's easy for you to say. You're not so fat."

"I'm up here, aren't I?"

"Yeah, but you don't have a hundred pounds to lose."

"Langer wants you to lose a hundred pounds this summer?"

Julius shook his head. "My dad wants me to."

"I don't think it's even possible. Maybe in a year . . ."

"Maybe in a century," Julius scoffed. "I'm not cut

out to be thin. It's one of those goals like reading the
Bible cover-to-cover. It's something you'd like to do,
but you know you'll never get around to it."

"Langer would say that's a lousy attitude."

"That's exactly what he said. Who cares? You can't
get anything extra to eat up here no matter what
your attitude is."

"That reminds me," I said, lowering my voice.
"What'd you do with the, uh, junk from last night?"

"Ate it."

"Seriously."

"Down the crapper."

"Good work."

"Let's hustle, men!" Maury yelled, slapping us on
the back and scaring us to the brink of heart failure.
"We'll be late for our swim!"

He ran ahead. Julius and I did our best to pretend
he couldn't possibly have understood what we were
talking about.

6

They had special names for everything at this camp. "Slimnastics," which was a polite way of saying "exercises." "Swim 'n' trim," which for me was a polite way of saying "paddling around in the shallow end and getting yelled at by the swim coach." And "portion control," which was a polite way of saying "starving."

The hour after lunch was called "active rest." Your counselor hung around the cabin to make sure nobody dozed off. When you're awake, as Maury carefully pointed out, you burn up twice as many calories as when you're asleep. I burned up mine composing love poems to chocolate chocolate-chip ice cream.

As for "free activity," it offered about as much freedom as everything else at camp. On Monday I picked archery, but archery was full, so I had to take crafts, which was about my least favorite thing in the world. Maury insisted I'd get my chance to shoot a bow and arrow on Wednesday. Of course, it rained Wednesday.

It also rained Thursday. Our cabin wasn't heated, and the cool dampness came through the windows and the boards and made my skin crawl. And I was starving. And the cabin reeked of Lysol and puke. On Tuesday, brilliant historian Howard Andeker had informed us that the Indians used to survive on honeysuckle, and to prove it he'd wolfed down so much of the stuff that he barfed all over the cabin floor.

When it rained, it poured boredom. Duff demonstrated how to fold your ear and more interesting parts of your anatomy. Julius and Nick leg-wrestled on the floor, with the loser landing in the spot where Howard had puked. And we played strip poker. I lost and wound up having to run down to the latrine and back in my birthday suit, much to everyone's amusement. It was pretty humiliating and I got drenched, but I took a little revenge by drying off with Nick's sheets. After which I had the horrible feeling I'd been invaded by cooties.

What I missed most was contact with the world outside this loony bin. I wrote to my friend Sloss, but I really didn't expect to hear from him, since the last time I went to camp I wrote him twice and he never wrote back. Claimed he was too busy loafing around.

The only thing I got in the mail was a letter from my parents describing all the wonderful restaurants they'd stopped at on their way home. After going on and on in loving detail about every bite, they promised they'd take me to a couple of the places after camp. Needless to say, instead of making me look forward to some delicious meals a month and a half away, it just made me feel rotten about all the terrible food I'd be swallowing for the next six weeks. In fact, I nearly ate the letter. It couldn't've tasted any worse than our cheese sandwiches.

Otherwise, aside from the local paper (whose big headline PRIZE STEER DISAPPEARS; SUSPECTS SOUGHT made me wonder if some of my fellow campers had organized a secret barbecue), my one contact with reality was my portable radio. In the daytime, all you could get on it was six-month-old rock music and the Hundred and One Strings playing Lawrence Welk and country singers raining tears in their beers. But at night, things got better. Yoi could pull in stations from the big cities.

The only problem was that we weren't supposed to play our radios after lights out, which was the only time you could hear anything good. I risked it anyway, using the earphone to avoid getting caught. I was slightly worried I might fall asleep and get strangled by the cord, since my mother always insisted she once read about this happening to some kid, but I decided to chance it.

I pulled in Boston clear as a bell, and some French stations from Quebec, and some country music from down South. Mostly, though, it was rock, but at least it was more or less up to date. But the best thing was baseball. I couldn't get the Phillies' station, but I did find a couple of their games on the other teams' broadcasts. It was weird listening to the announcers root against my team.

Anyway, I really liked fooling around with my

radio at night. Then we had the radio war. During the rain on Thursday, Nick tuned his radio to that rotten station that played what it called the top forty but was more like the top five from six months ago. He played it loud and refused to turn it down, which meant there was no way I could do any reading, so I got out my radio and played the country station.

Nick turned his radio up louder. So did I. About the time our eardrums were ready to surrender, Duff got into the act and turned on Lawrence Welk and all those strings. Then my station started playing Bernie Androsky's favorite song, "The Trucker Named Bodine." Androsky snatched up Nick's radio and Duff's and shut them off. Nick couldn't catch him, so he grabbed my radio instead.

"Damn it!" I screamed, as the singer went on about how this guy kept his tractor clean. "Give it back!"

"Make Androsky give me mine."

"Make him yourself. I want my radio."

Nick held it at arm's length, just out of my reach. "Here it is. Take it."

"Wide as a truck, don't press your luck with the trucker named Bodine," sang the radio. I lunged at it, but Nick swung it away.

"Come on. Here it is."

I reached for it again as the radio sang *big and fat and mean.* Nick swung it away from me and made a quick move toward Androsky. My radio hit Duff's bunk and crashed to the floor. You could hear it crack all the way to Taiwan.

"You son of a bitch, Barris!" I screamed. I knew the radio must be ruined, but I picked it up to see if it still would play. It wouldn't. "This radio cost me twenty dollars!" I shouted.

"I didn't break it," Nick said calmly, as if the thing had magically walked off my bunk. "You did."

"Come on. Is there anybody here who doesn't think Nick broke my radio?"

Nobody answered. "Okay, Nick," I said. "Twenty dollars." I stuck out my hand.

"Where am I going to get money?"

"I don't care where you get it. I want my money."

"I don't know what you're talking about. We're not allowed to have money up here."

I knew that, of course, but I didn't let it bother me. "I want my money," I said again. My neck muscles were chafing against my T-shirt. I could feel how red I was, and only part of it was my sunburn.

"I want a rocket ship, but Santa isn't going to bring me one," Nick said.

It was one of those situations where you all of a sudden forget yourself and all your manners and civilization and everything and you don't even think. You just feel as though the only way you're going to make any progress is to punch somebody in the mouth, and the next thing you know, you've done it. And then this fear rushes up into your throat because you realize it was a super-stupid thing to do

40

and you have no idea what's going to happen next.

Nick swung back, but I stepped away, and the next thing I knew, two hundred-odd pounds of flab were diving toward me. Nick and I fell to the floor, and he started punching me in the face, and I could hear the other guys yelling something I couldn't make out, and I tried to get out from under him, but it wasn't working at all, and I could feel the back of my head scraping against a splinter or a nail or something on the floor when he punched me again, and I hit him in the face a couple of times, but not very hard since I didn't have room to wind up, and finally I could see Julius push Nick off me and I gasped and panted and wheezed and tried to catch my breath.

Maury came through the door. "Okay, who started this?"

I pointed to Nick and gasped his last name.

"What's this all about?" Maury demanded.

"Nothing much," Nick sneered.

"That bastard broke my radio," I panted, sticking a word between each breath. A trickle of blood ran down the back of my neck.

"Did you?" Maury asked Nick.

Nick shrugged. "Hell, no."

"Like hell you didn't," said Julius.

"It dropped while we were messing around," Nick said.

"It dropped while *you* were messing around. After you stole it from me," I said.

Nick didn't say anything.

41

"It cost me twenty bucks," I said, "and I want it fixed."

"Where's Nick going to get money up here?" Maury asked.

"What you ought to do," Andeker said, "is make Barris give his radio to Zimmer."

"Yeah," I said. "How about that?"

"What do you say, Barris?" Maury asked.

"I say it stinks."

"That's the only fair thing," I said.

Maury looked exasperated. "Look, Zimmer, there's a limit to what I can do. I can't just take Barris's radio away from him."

"Why not?"

"It's his personal property, that's why not."

"You said you could take our food if we had any."

"That's different. There's a camp rule that says a counselor's supposed to confiscate any food he finds. There's no camp rule that says a counselor is supposed to give Barris's radio to Zimmer. Look, I'll lend you mine some of the time."

"When?"

"Whenever you want."

"How about tonight?"

"Sure, till lights out."

"All night."

"There's no radio after lights out. What're you going to do with it? Sleep on it?"

"Play with it," Nick smirked.

"That's enough out of you, Barris," Maury said. "You two shake hands."

"Aw, come on," Nick said.

"Some other time," I mumbled. I felt like the inside of a sewer.

"Now," said Maury. "Or you two can stay down here and iron out your differences while the rest of us eat lunch."

At those magic words, Nick stuck his hand out as if it were jet-propelled. There wasn't much I could do but go along. Nick crunched my fingers a little just to let me know who'd won that round. Then Maury helped me clean up my wounds.

We all put on our raincoats and slogged up the muddy path to the mess hall. I couldn't look anybody in the eye, so I looked down at our tracks. They were good and deep. After nearly a week of slimming down, we still weren't exactly feathers.

As usual after lunch, Miss Shirt read off our weights, and one of the camp staffers posted them. "Barris, 197," she said. "Nice work, Nick. Schwartz, 188. See, you can do it, Frank. Zimmer, 167. Boy, if you keep this up, we'll have to tie you down to keep you from blowing away."

"They might have to tie you down to keep you from beating people up," Nick snorted. I pretended I didn't hear.

"House, 224. Better get on the ball, Julius. Gotta lose those three pounds for tomorrow, or there goes your privilege for the week."

Julius sort of half grinned. It's about the only thing you can do when somebody humiliates you in public like that. He was the only person in the whole camp who hadn't lost a pound. Of course, we all knew why.

When Miss Shirt finished with the list, she yelled, "How do you feel?"

We were all supposed to holler back "Terrific!" It was the feeblest "Terrific!" you ever heard, and it was mixed in with a lot of "Rotten!" and "Hungry!" and "Awful!"

Dr. Langer got up on the platform and took the mike. "A lot of you have been asking what the special privilege is this week. Well, you're all making such excellent progress, I've decided to announce it. At seven-thirty this Saturday night, we're going to have our very first camp-wide activity." He paused for effect. "A dance."

Some of the counselors and a few of the kids applauded. Everybody else kept quiet.

"Some privilege," said Russell Duff.

"I told you day before yesterday. Believe me once in a while," said Frank Schwartz.

"They have refreshments at these dances?" Nick wondered.

"Oh, sure," Frank said.

"Potato chips?"

"What's a potato chip?" Howard Andeker snorted.

"A fossil," I said. "Completely extinct in this part of New Hampshire."

"What kind of refreshments *do* we get?" asked Russ Duff.

"Celery sticks. Carrots. Stuff like that," Frank said.

"I wonder if you can overdose on carrots," Julius said.

"You won't overdose on anything," Nick pointed out. "You're gonna be down in the cabin playing with yourself."

"Who says?" Julius shot back.

"Miss Shirt up there."

"I still could lose those pounds," Julius said.

"Yeah," laughed Nick Barris. "And it could rain Hershey bars tonight."

7

"That scale can't be right," Julius said. "Let me try again."

He stepped off and stepped on again. The scale didn't cooperate. He still weighed exactly the same as he had at the beginning of the week.

"Dr. Langer wants to see you first thing after breakfast," Maury informed him. So after we had our usual scrumptious morning meal, Julius stayed behind.

"All right, guys, where is it?" Maury asked the rest of us when we got back to the cabin.

Nobody said a word.

"Where's what?" Russell Duff finally asked.

"Come on. Where's House hiding his food?"

No reply.

"I really don't like to have to do this," Maury said. He dragged Julius's trunk from under the bed. It was locked.

"That's his private property," I said.

"Not if he's hiding food in it, it isn't." Maury took out an enormous ring with every sort of key you could possibly imagine. He stared at the lock on Julius's trunk, and then he started trying keys on it.

46

"I hate this," he said. "Makes me feel like a burglar. But it's for your benefit."

"Why do you think he has food?" Bernie asked.

"Come on, Androsky. You can't maintain your weight on what we feed you. It's impossible."

"Maybe he's been hitting the honeysuckle," said Nick Barris. Andeker kicked him.

Maury finally found a key that fit the lock, but it wouldn't turn. Disgusted, he slapped the trunk and tried another key. That one worked. Maury opened the trunk.

Julius's empty duffel bag was in the tray on top, which Maury lifted out. Beneath it were socks and shorts. Beneath them were T-shirts stuffed with magazines. Sex magazines. Maury riffled through a couple and shook his head.

"The guy's been holding out on us," Nick snickered.

Beneath the magazines, Maury found what he was after: cartons of candy, the kind stores buy, with a couple dozen bars per box. Tootsie Pops, Snickers, Three Musketeers, Milky Ways, more Tootsie Pops, Jujyfruits, Butterfingers, and Baby Ruths. "Any of you know about these?" Maury scowled.

Nobody said anything. Maury piled the candy boxes on top of the magazines and carried them out the door.

"Jesus!" said Russell Duff, checking to make sure Maury was out of earshot. "I'm glad that wasn't my stuff."

"Where'd those magazines go?" Nick asked.

"He took them," I said.

"You can't get fat reading magazines," Duff said.

"You don't read those magazines," Howard Andeker said. "You look at them."

"Well, I wouldn't mind looking," Nick said.

"Me, neither," said Duff.

"Anybody else got any?" Nick asked.

Nobody did.

We were changing into our swimsuits when Julius got back. It didn't take him long to notice his open footlocker in the middle of the floor. "Hell!" he shouted, stooping down to examine the damage. "He took my magazines!"

"Serves you right," Nick said. "You should've shared them."

"I mean, I had it coming for the candy. But the magazines aren't any of his business."

"Dirty magazines," said Bernie Androsky.

"It's a free country," Julius said.

"Not for kids," Frank Schwartz droned.

"Besides, Camp Thin-na-Yet seceded from the United States," Andeker said. "We're part of Slobbovia."

Julius kept shaking his head as he pawed through his trunk. "Jeez! I just don't believe this!"

"What'd Langer say?" I asked him.

"Aw, you know. Bad attitude. Dishonesty. Change my habits. Et cetera. Do I want to be fat and ugly the rest of my life?"

"Do you?" Nick asked.

"I can think of a few fat people who did okay."

"Like who?"

"President William Howard Taft. Alfred Hitchcock. Babe Ruth. The guy who played Cannon on TV. Kate Smith."

"Kate Smith!" Howard Andeker sneered.

Julius ignored him. "Jackie Gleason. Sarah Caldwell."

"Who?" Nick demanded.

"The director of the Boston Opera, churl," said Howard Andeker.

"Luciano Pavarotti. Orson Welles. Lots of people."

"Maybe you should start a camp for people who want to be fat," said Franklin Schwartz.

"I don't want to be fat," Julius said. "All I'm saying is that it's not the only thing in life to worry about."

"Ha! Tell that to Langer!" I said.

"I did. You know what he said? 'I agree with you one hundred percent. We're just trying to get you to realize that it *is* a problem.' You know what I said? I said, 'Maybe you should conk us on the head with a frozen turkey to make your point.'"

Maury stepped through the door. "You know the rules, House. No lunch today."

Julius shrugged.

"And you're down here for the evening while we're up at the dance."

"That's not news," Julius said. "Where are my magazines?"

49

"Which magazines?"

"You know which magazines."

"Oh, *those* magazines. I picked them up along with the candy."

"How about bringing them back? They don't have any calories."

"Maybe your mother'd like to know what kind of crap you read."

"My mother's dead."

Maury frowned. "Your father, then."

"He doesn't care what I read."

"Well, we do. You guys have no business looking at that stuff."

"Of course, you counselors never look at those kinds of pictures," sniffed Howard Andeker.

"What we do is none of your business," Maury answered testily. "We're all over eighteen. You guys aren't."

"If you don't give those magazines back, I'm going to get Langer to make you give 'em back," Julius said.

"Try it," Maury snarled. He had a vicious look on his face. "Just try it, pal." He looked like he might slug somebody.

"I will," Julius muttered. Fortunately, I was the only one who heard him.

Maury exhaled. "All right," he said "Everybody down to the lake." He strode out the door.

"I'll get those books back," Julius said.

"Yeah, when baseballs grow toenails," Nick scoffed.

"I'm telling you, I'll get 'em back."

"How?" Duff asked.

"For me to know and you to find out," Julius said. That more or less settled the issue for a while. When the rest of us got back to the cabin after lunch, Julius asked me what he'd missed.

"Oxygen sandwiches," I said. "And cow pies."

"No kidding."

"And after Dr. Langer explained once again how, ounce for ounce, bread has fewer calories than meat, Miss Shirt crowned the King and Queen of Thin."

"You weren't in the running," Nick jibed.

"You know, Nick," Julius said, "sometime that mouth of yours is going to open once too often."

Before Nick had a chance to think up a comeback, Franklin Schwartz announced that he felt terrible. And while we made jokes about the various diseases he might have, he passed out on the floor.

8

We weren't allowed to visit Frank in the infirmary. The official word from Maury was that there didn't seem to be anything seriously wrong with him, but they were keeping him under observation just in case. "That's what they said right before my mother died," Julius announced, just to cheer everybody up.

"What it is," Howard Andeker sniffed, "is an open-and-shut case of malnutrition."

We all spent a lot of time combing our hair and tying our ties and stuff for the dance, since it was supposed to be a big deal with jackets and everything even though the temperature and the humidity were both in the nineties and the mess hall wasn't air-conditioned and when it filled up with fat dancing bodies it'd probably get so steamy it'd cause a mass deodorant failure. Under the circumstances, Julius didn't seem all that unhappy not to be going.

The decoration committee had actually done a halfway decent job with the mess hall. The place was darker than usual, with long waves of blue and yellow crepe paper dangling from the ceiling. The tables were all pushed down to the kitchen end, where some of them were set with big trays of carrots, celery, tomatoes, lettuce, and pickles, and punch bowls with tigers' heads spitting bug juice.

Most of the girls sat along the far wall. Nick and Howard plunged right in and found partners, but Androsky and Duff and I and quite a few others stood around the refreshment tables and watched. "You gonna ask anybody?" Duff hollered over the music.

"Maybe next number," I said, trying to work up a little courage. I had a fluttery feeling in my stomach. Normally I didn't have to worry about girls. I just took it for granted that they found me pretty unappetizing. Sometimes I didn't have to take it for granted—they told me so right to my face. Now for once I had a chance to meet some girls who might sympathize with me and my hyperactive appetite, and I didn't know what to do. Besides, most of the girls standing against the wall looked so mopey and forlorn they didn't seem worth asking. I mean, even fat people have standards.

I kept looking for that girl with the gorgeous gray eyes. She sat at the table next to ours in the mess hall, and from some of the things I'd overheard her say, she sounded kind of interesting. I finally spotted her on the dance floor with an older guy. She danced pretty well, which kind of scared me. But when the number ended, she leaned against the wall, took out a memo pad, and wrote something down. I didn't see anybody going after her, so I walked over and asked her to dance.

"I'm tired of dancing," she yelled as the music started.

I wasn't sure if she was rejecting me or not, so I hung around.

"What's your name?" she shouted.

I told her. Her mouth moved again, but I couldn't hear her over the music. "Huh?" I said.

"Clean out your ears, bozo!"

I moved my finger around in my ear. "Try again!"

"Belinda Moss. Got it?"

I nodded. "Belinda. You don't want to dance?"

She shook her head. "Let's get something to eat."

We made our way to the food table. "Grab some stuff," she said, "and let's go outside."

We each took a fistful of celery and carrots and pickles and headed for the door. A counselor was guarding it. "What's wrong?" she asked us.

"Too noisy in here," Belinda yelled through a mouthful of celery. "Our ears need to recover."

"I'm not supposed to let anybody out," the counselor said.

"What is this, a dance or a dungeon?" Belinda shouted.

"We don't want anybody to get into trouble, that's all."

"Don't worry," Belinda said. "There's no food outside."

"I've got my orders," the woman said. "Why don't you just relax and enjoy the dance?"

Belinda turned away. "The hell with her," she shouted in my ear. "Follow me!"

I followed her to the far corner of the refreshment table. Belinda made sure nobody was looking, then sneaked under the table and crawled into the kitchen. I stayed right behind her. Once we were out of sight, we stood up and went out the back door.

"Free at last!" she cried, as we stepped out into the fresh night air.

I always feel guilty about breaking rules. Even dumb ones. "What do you think they'll do if they find us?" I wondered.

"What can they do? Cut off your food? Not let you go to the next wonderful sweaty dance? Big deal."

"You sound like you really love this place."

"I get so mad sometimes. I mean, the whole idea that you have to stay put in the mess hall. They treat us like prisoners."

"We *are* prisoners."

"For violation of camp rules, I hereby sentence you to six weeks on bread and water. Minus the bread: fattening, you know," she said in a Nazi accent. "Come on, let's do something to get back at these jerks."

"Like what?"

"God! Of all the people I could be out here with, I have to get stuck with somebody with no imagination. Think!"

I thought. I never was good at mischief. The only thing I could imagine was setting the whole camp on fire, but that would probably burn down a perfectly good forest and half the state of New Hampshire and send me to prison for arson and murder, and even if it didn't I'd have a life sentence of guilt. It was so dumb I didn't even want to say it out loud. "I'm stumped," I said.

"I can see who's going to be the brains of this outfit," Belinda said. "Look, there are all sorts of things we could do. We could sneak back into the kitchen and raid the refrigerators."

"They're locked. Besides, there's nothing in them but foilfood anyway."

"Well, at least you're observant."

"Would you mind being a little less sarcastic?"

"Sorry. That's what my homeroom teacher calls my 'abrasive style.' I'm like that with everybody. My Mom says that's why I don't have more friends."

"Maybe she's right."

"Look, I don't enjoy being insulted myself. Truce?"

"Sure."

"Okay. Back to business," Belinda said. "We're out here all alone without anybody looking over our shoulders, while everybody else is in there pretending to have a good time. What say we stage a little raid on the supply depot, pardner?"

"The counselors' mess? The cooks'll be in there."

"How about one of the counselors' cabins?"

"What if we get caught?"

She gave me a very exasperated look. "What's the

very worst they could do? Send you home, right? Horrible!"

"They could starve you for a week or something."

"Then we could report them to the authorities for abusing a minor child. Big trouble, abuse of a minor child. I've studied some law. Besides, we're not going to get caught. Every single counselor is in the mess hall. There's nobody to catch us." She took out her memo pad. "See? I've got a checklist. Nobody's out here but us, unless some other kids sneaked away before we did. Now, are we going to raid the counselors' cabins or not?"

"There're four of them," I pointed out. "Which one would we raid?"

"How about the one your counselor's in?"

"Great. That ought to get me a gold medal if we get caught."

"I told you, we're not going to get caught," Belinda assured me. "Besides, if we do, we'll be in a lot less trouble in a men's cabin than a women's."

"How do you figure that?"

"The old double standard. Sugar and spice, that's what little girls are made of. You guys are full of snips and snails and rotten stuff. If they found you in the girls' counselors' cabin, they'd think you were some kind of pervert, hung up on sniffing panties or something, and Langer would make you go to special therapy sessions for weeks. Guys are supposed to have these uncontrollable urges. But if they found me in a men's cabin, they wouldn't think of accusing

57

me of anything weird. We females are supposed to be above that sort of thing."

"Are you?"

"Are you kidding?" She laughed. "Look, we don't have forever. Are you coming or not?"

"I guess so."

"Okay, Scout! Lead the way!"

9

This may sound goofy, but somehow when we slinked around the mess hall and across the volleyball court and down the path, I actually felt romantic. It was getting really dark out, and when the path narrowed, Belinda grabbed my hand. It made me shiver. The only girl who'd ever held my hand before was my cousin Jane when she was too little to cross the street by herself.

Just in case Belinda'd forgotten somebody on her list, we didn't say a word to each other, which for some reason made my heart beat even faster with all sorts of ideas of closeness and love and stuff. But when we reached the clearing, Belinda was all business. "Where's their cabin?" she whispered.

It was so dark we could hardly see a thing. All I could make out of the cabin was one corner. Our planning hadn't been too super. We'd overlooked the fact that with all the lanterns up at the mess hall, the cabins would be as dark as our insides. "How are we going to raid the cabin when we can hardly even see it?" I wondered.

Belinda didn't answer.

"Well?" I demanded.

59

"Give me a break, huh? I'm thinking." Then all of a sudden she grabbed my arm and took a step back. "What's that?" she whispered.

"What?"

She pointed down the hill. Lantern light moved out from the latrine and up along the path toward my cabin. It didn't take me long to figure out whose waddle was propelling the light along.

"Julius!" I hissed. He didn't hear me.

"Are you crazy?" Belinda whispered.

"It's okay," I said, pulling her by the hand. We followed Julius up to the cabin steps. Humming to himself, he never heard us until I whispered his name again.

"Jesus!" he cried, turning around. "If I hadn't just gone to the john, you'd've scared the crap out of me!"

"Belinda Moss, this is Julius House," I said.

"You here to mess around or something?" Julius asked.

"We need that lantern," Belinda said.

"You can mess around in the dark."

"We're not messing around," I said. "We're raiding the counselors' cabin."

"Great," Belinda said. "Why don't you tell the whole camp about it?"

"Julius is okay," I said. "He won't tell on us."

"Sure he will," Belinda said, " 'cause he'll get blamed for it. He's been down here all night, and everybody else is supposed to be at the dance, so he's the prime suspect."

"Right," Julius agreed. "So I may as well go along. No sense getting blamed for something I didn't do."

"Well, it's nice to meet somebody with gumption," Belinda said, shooting a significant look at me. I began to wonder whether letting Julius in on this was such a hot idea after all. But it was too late now to tell him to take a hike, and besides, he had the lantern.

We all marched over to the counselors' cabin. Julius stood guard at the bottom of the stairs while Belinda and I climbed up to the porch with the lantern. I tried the door.

"Locked," I said.

"What did you expect?" Belinda sniffed. "They're not supposed to make it easy on us prowlers." She took the lantern and inspected the door. "I can open some locks with a piece of cardboard, but that one's a deadbolt. No way."

"Now what?" I wondered.

"Some burglar you are," Belinda said. "What we do now is check out the windows." She shone the lantern in a little window beside the door at about the level of our heads.

"How's it coming?" Julius asked.

"The window's open, but there's a screen on it," I said. "It won't budge."

"So cut it. Got a knife?"

"No."

"I'll go back to the cabin and get mine," Julius said. Belinda handed him the lantern.

"Do they teach thief courses in your school?" I asked her while we waited.

"Come on, Zimmer. Except for my weight, I'm your basic average normal kid, only smarter. This isn't theft. This is war."

"I've never been a big war fan," I said. I was really nervous. I'm usually the kind of ridiculously honest person who pays adult price at the movies the day he turns twelve—well, not too long after, anyway—and this was my first attempt at burglary.

Julius came back. "I'll cut the screen," he said. "This knife cost me plenty, and I don't want it getting dull. Here."

He handed me the lantern and thrust the knife into the screen. It offered so little resistance that his arm went right through the open window. "Plastic," he said, shaking his head. A couple more cuts and the job was done.

"Okay, Zimmer, get in there," Belinda commanded.

"Me? Why me?"

"You're the only one who can fit."

One advantage of being "thin," I told myself. I handed her the lantern and my suit jacket, and then I put my hands on the windowsill and pulled. Julius boosted me from behind, and somehow I managed to squirm halfway through. That's when I could hear my pants tearing on some splinters.

The first thing I thought of was, "There goes your only suit." The second thing was, "We'll never get away with this."

"What's the holdup?" Julius asked impatiently.

"I'm trying to find a place to land." Dropping headfirst from the window didn't seem too bright, so I grabbed the end of a top bunk, crawled onto it, and hopped down from there. It was pitch black inside.

First I nearly broke my neck on whatever was sticking out in the middle of the floor. Somebody's trunk; evidently the neatness "suggestions" didn't apply to counselors. Then I felt along the wall with my hands, trying to find the door and the lock knob. No luck. Then Belinda got an inspiration and held the lantern through the window. That made it easy.

I opened the door. Belinda came around with the lantern. I checked my pants; they were snagged a little. Nothing serious.

"You keep watch," Julius told Belinda, handing her the lantern.

"What? This whole thing was my idea!"

"But this is a guys' cabin," he protested. "Maybe there's stuff in there you're not supposed to see."

"Well, I'll try not to be too shocked," she laughed, and stormed in past me.

"God, what a mess!" she cried. She wasn't kidding. Talk about pigsties. The inside of this cabin looked like the set of a disaster movie. Only worse. Underwear hung from the rafters, socks drooped over the bedrails, newspapers lined the floor, little trails of ants marched into empty soda cans. And not one of the beds was made. No wonder the place was off-limits to campers.

But the thing that made it absolutely off-limits was

the wallpaper. It wasn't your standard pattern. It was foldouts of naked women the counselors had tacked up every which way. I sort of tried to look and not look at the same time.

"Disgusting," Belinda said, staring at the pictures.

"I thought you weren't going to be shocked," Julius said.

"I'm not. I'm disgusted."

"Come on. You must've looked at yourself in the mirror once in a while."

"That's what I mean. I'm disgusted at how gorgeous they are. Look at her! God, I'd give anything to have thighs like that!"

I could just feel the counselors' footsteps coming down the hill. "Look, let's get going. We've got to get out of here before somebody finds us."

"Well, there's the food supply," Belinda said, pointing to a refrigerator.

"And it's padlocked shut," I observed.

Foiled again! But it didn't faze Belinda.

"Sometimes you can open those locks with a safety pin," she said. "I'll see what I can do. You guys look in their drawers for snack food."

"I don't know whether we should do that," I mumbled.

"They went through my stuff, didn't they?" Julius said. "Hey, I wonder where Maury would've put my magazines."

"Look for food," Belinda commanded. "You can't eat magazines."

64

I tried a drawer. It was full of tangled, unmatched socks. The next drawer was stuffed with underwear. Below that, I found sweaters and sweatshirts. Not a crumb of food.

"Aha!" Julius cried. He'd found his magazines in Maury's bottom drawer.

"Listen, I can't get that fridge open," Belinda said, "but there must be food out here someplace. These guys are too slobby to put it away all the time."

Julius helped me aim the lantern into the back corners of the top shelves. We thought they might be hiding food there. They weren't.

We inspected every cranny of the footlockers. There wasn't a morsel to be found. We were totally out of luck.

"Now what?" I asked the master thief.

"I don't know about you guys," Julius said, "but I'm taking my magazines."

"Don't be a moron," Belinda said. "If they find those things missing, they'll accuse you for sure."

"I don't care. I'm taking them with me."

"Then there's only one thing to do," Belinda said. "We'll have to take all the rest, too."

"Why?" I asked.

"At least that way it won't look like muttonhead here broke in just to get his. It'll divert suspicion. And it'll drive them nuts. We can destroy the evidence."

"I'm not destroying my magazines," Julius insisted, shoving them firmly under his arm.

Belinda started ripping pictures from the wall. "Dimwit, if they find you with those magazines, they'll put you in solitary for a week."

"I'm keeping my magazines."

"Zimmer, tell him how stupid he's acting," Belinda said, as she ripped a luscious body from the wall.

"She's right," I said.

"I'm keeping them," Julius insisted.

Belinda shrugged. "Suit yourself."

We stripped the walls down to the wood and gathered up all the sex magazines we could find. "What I can't figure out is why guys like to look at this stuff so much," Belinda said. "What's such a big deal about women's bodies?"

"In your case, nothing," Julius said.

"God, look who's talking! The Goodyear blimp!"

"Look," I said, "save the insults for later. We've got to get back up there to that dance."

As Belinda and I carried our stacks of magazines out the door, Julius held the lantern. "All I can say," I told him, "is you better have those magazines out of sight by the time we get back from the dance." He didn't seem worried about it.

"Nice meeting you," he told Belinda, "even if you are weird."

"Same here," Belinda said.

The path to the mess hall was darker than ever. Belinda and I made our way up the hill. By the light from the dance, we sneaked across the volley-ball court. I set down my magazines and lifted the heavy metal lid of a big trash bin. Belinda dumped in all the magazines and I let the lid down easy.

"Mission accomplished," she said, dusting off her hands.

"Not exactly," I reminded her. "No food." Actually, I felt a little stupid about what we'd done. But I also felt a little proud, mainly because it was the first time since I'd been up here that I'd done anything at all without a bunch of counselors or coaches looking over my shoulder.

Belinda was standing there smiling at me. Somehow she looked a lot more beautiful than all those beauties in the counselors' foldouts. I wanted to kiss her, but I wasn't exactly an expert on the subject. My only experience with such things was a quick peck on the cheek from Dulcie Ripstein at a party where I got roped into playing spin-the-bottle. The only thing I could remember about it was the flavor of partially digested onions.

I put one arm around Belinda's shoulder and touched my lips to hers. She moved closer, and we held each other. She was warm and comfortable and smelled like some kind of soap my grandmother used to use, and without saying anything she was teaching me a couple of things about kissing when somebody whispered, "Hey! What's going on out there?"

Belinda backed away from me and smoothed her hair.

"Fast worker, aren't you?" Nick Barris said from the kitchen steps.

"You worry about your problems," I said, straightening my tie.

"I got no problems," Nick said. He and a girl came toward us. "Who's your friend?" he smirked.

"Look, Nick, we've got to get back inside," I said. "See you later."

"At least introduce me."

"This is Belinda Moss. Belinda, Nick Barris."

Nick made a little bow. "Delighted."

"Yeah, me, too," Belinda said. "See you." She pulled me toward the kitchen.

"What's your hurry?" Nick yelled, but the girl with him said, "Leave them alone."

"What a creep!" Belinda said once we were in the kitchen. She pecked me on the cheek. Then she slid under the refreshment tables. I followed her.

The scene at the dance was pretty much what I'd expected. Boogieing with the blue cabin's counselor, Miss Shirt was the center of attention and loved every minute of it. Howard Andeker was on the floor with a big, clumsy blonde who kept bumping into people. Bernie Androsky was having a hard time trying to convince a frizzy-haired butterball to dance with him. Russ Duff loitered beside the refreshment table with a carrot stick dangling from his mouth.

"Where the hell have *you* been?" he growled, but before I could answer him, Langer was on the P.A.

68

system asking if everybody'd had a good time. Everybody sort of feebled back, "Yeah," and naturally Langer had to say, "I can't hear you," and after a couple more tries we mustered up a "Yeah" that was loud enough to suit him, and he announced the last dance. It was a slow one, and they turned the lights way down, and Belinda and I danced so close that when we passed Russ Duff he nearly choked on his carrot stick.

10

The first thing that happened after the dance was that our cabin stood around outside the mess hall waiting for Nick to show up. Nobody knew where he was, or at least nobody was telling. And a girl was missing, too.

Maury was angry. Having one of his campers suddenly disappear made him look bad. Langer took him aside and talked to him about it. While they were frowning and gesticulating, Bernie asked me, "Where is Nick, anyhow?"

"I don't have the foggiest idea," I lied. But it really wasn't all that much of a lie. Nick and his sweetheart could be anywhere by now.

"Probably whacking off somewhere," Andeker muttered.

"I wish he'd hurry up," Duff said, ripping off his tie. "I want to get out of this sweat suit."

Maury decided Nick ought to have enough sense to find his way back to the cabin, so we all started down the path. "Heard anything about Frank Schwartz?" I asked him.

"Right now, I'm more concerned about Barris." Now that Frank was in the infirmary, Maury considered him somebody else's worry.

There was a big commotion at the clearing. Lanterns were flying every which way. Counselors' voices boomed back and forth. "Hey, Tom, what's up?" Maury shouted to the nearest lantern.

"Some clown broke into our cabin."

"Aw, hell!" Maury said.

"Not polite," Andeker chided. Maury gave him a nasty look.

A lantern came toward us with a grim face behind it. Maury asked what happened, and the face mumbled an answer quietly enough so the rest of us couldn't hear. Maury shook his head angrily. "I think I can clear this up pretty quick," he muttered. The other lantern walked away.

"Did they take anything?" Duff asked. "Like food?"

Maury didn't bother to answer. He just stalked on ahead and up the stairs to our cabin. We stayed close behind.

Julius was lying on the bed, listening to Duff's radio and reading one of my comics, when Maury burst through the door. "How was the dance?" Julius asked in a pretty convincing tone.

"Where were you all evening?" Maury demanded.

"Where does it look like?"

"I don't know. Somebody broke into the counselors' cabin while the rest of us were having fun."

"Well, it wasn't me."

"Then who was it?"

"How should I know? Nobody asked me to guard your cabin."

"Nobody asked you to break into it, either."

"Don't you think it'd be awfully stupid and obvious of me to break into your cabin when I'm the only one who's supposed to be down here?"

"It was awfully stupid and obvious of you to hide that candy of yours all week, too."

Julius grinned. "I'll bet the candy was a lot more fun than the dance."

"Hear, hear," said Russell Duff.

"House, I can't prove it's you," Maury said. "Yet. But if I find out you're the one who did it, you'd better lock yourself in your trunk and throw away the key." Maury stormed out of the cabin.

"What'd you steal?" Andeker asked, once Maury was out of earshot.

"Your mother's panties," Julius said. "There was a pair in every counselor's drawer."

"You better take that back, House."

"Check that. Two pairs."

"I'm warning you . . ."

"Lay off, Andeker. You wouldn't hit a man with an empty stomach."

Sweaty and breathless, Nick Barris stepped through the door. "Hey," he panted, "why didn't somebody tell me the dance was over?"

"We wanted to see how much trouble you'd get into," Andeker said.

"Well, whatever it is, it was worth it," Nick smirked.

"Just to kiss a pig?" Andeker asked.

Maury rushed through the door again. "All right, House! Where are they?"

"I know he's fat, but I don't think you should count Nick as two people," Julius said calmly. "He's right here."

Maury looked toward him. "I'll talk to you later, Barris." He turned back to Julius. "Open your trunk."

"You already took all my candy," Julius said.

"Open it up, wiseguy."

"Open it yourself," Julius said. "It's not locked."

Maury flung open the footlocker and rummaged through it. What he found was what he'd seen the other day, minus the candy and magazines and a couple of pieces of underwear. All I could see of him was the back of his neck, but even that looked angry.

He slammed the trunk shut and started going through Julius's drawers. He didn't find anything special there, either. "I don't know where you put that trash, House, but when I find out . . ."

"Will somebody please tell me what's going on?" Nick asked.

"Somebody broke into the counselors' cabin," Bernie said.

"Who?" Nick asked. "House?"

Suddenly Maury's eyes lit up. He grabbed Julius's mattress and flipped it over. He must've thought he'd find the magazines between the mattress and the springs. A pretty good piece of detective work, except that all he found were fuzzy dustballs.

Maury stood there catching his breath. Then he turned to Nick. "Where were *you*, Barris?"

"Having fun," Nick replied in a cocky tone.

"What's that supposed to mean?"

"I got busy. Kind of lost track of the time."

"Where were you?"

"Out in the woods."

"With a girl?"

Nick glanced at me. I wondered what he'd say. "I wasn't the only one," he said.

"Nobody else was missing when the dance broke up," Maury said.

"Maybe some people went out and came back before the dance finished," Nick said, giving me a hard stare.

"Look, I don't want to hear about other people," Maury said. "I want to hear about what *you* were doing."

"You sure these babies are mature enough?" Nick smirked. "I might say something wrong in front of them."

"Get your footlocker out, Barris."

"Huh?"

"Come on. I want to see something."

"Huh?"

Maury yanked the trunk out from under Nick's bed. He opened it and rifled it. At the bottom, he found what he was looking for.

"Okay, Barris. Come with me."

"I don't get it," Nick said. "What's this all about?"

"You know damn well what it's about," Maury said, carefully taking out the magazines and using his elbow to hide the naked woman on the cover of the top one. "Let's go."

"Where'd that stuff come from?" Nick asked, exactly as though he'd known all along.

Maury pushed him out the door. "The rest of you guys, get ready for bed."

We could hear Nick protesting all the way to the counselors' cabin. It was the worst job of playing innocent I'd ever heard. Probably Nick had played innocent so many times, he didn't know what to do when he really *was* innocent.

"I wonder what they'll do to him," Russ Duff said.

"I wonder what he *did*," said Bernie Androsky.

And if Julius was wondering the same thing I was, he was wondering whether anybody would figure out who the real culprits were. Even for a dimwit like Nick, it shouldn't be all that hard.

The real question was what he'd say about me. After all, he had seen me outside the mess hall during the dance. Considering how he'd just about come right out and blabbed it when Maury started grilling him, I figured he wouldn't be any too likely to keep his mouth shut once he started getting the third degree.

Julius and I traded worried looks across the sink as we brushed our teeth. That's when Nick came back. The first thing he did was pound me on the shoulders so hard it made me choke. Then he did the same thing to Julius. Finally he stepped back a ways. "I don't know who double-crossed me," he said, "but whoever it was better watch out."

Julius charged him. That was why Nick had taken those steps back. He knew Julius would chase him, and he wasn't about to get caught. I was just about ready to join the chase myself when I realized that what Nick was saying meant he hadn't squealed on us.

I rinsed my teeth and pretended everything was normal. Julius gave up the chase.

"What did they do to you?" Duff asked Nick when he finally came back to the cabin.

"Nothing," Nick said.

"Horse manure!" Andeker scoffed.

"They must've done something," Duff insisted.

"I don't get any solid food tomorrow, is all," Nick said. "Big flaking deal."

"What else?" Andeker asked.

"No canteen for a week," Nick mumbled.

"Insignificant!" Andeker laughed.

"Actually, the only bad part is I have to take extra slimnastics for a week instead of free activity."

"We'll pray for you," Andeker promised.

"Next time, you ought to be a whole lot more careful who you steal from," Julius said smugly.

Nick threw a shoe at him. It hit me instead, and it didn't tickle. Nick's shoes were size seventy-three and weighed about eighteen pounds each.

11

F rank Schwartz still wasn't back next morning. We all wondered how he was doing. At the worst, he'd give us something interesting to write home about: "Dear Mom and Dad: The guy in the bunk across from me is a real bore. He hasn't said a word in two days. Maybe that's because he's dead."

Before we left for the mess hall, we all started talking about how special Sunday breakfast was supposed to be, just to make Nick feel worse about missing it. Actually, the only thing special about it turned out to be two strips of defatted, deflavored imitation bacon and half of a fossilized grapefruit with a plastic cherry on top. A real treat.

The only other unusual thing at breakfast was that Belinda accidentally on purpose dropped her napkin, and while she was bending over to pick it up, she slipped a note into my pocket. There was no way I could look at it without attracting a lot of attention, so I had to let it burn in my pants until I could get to someplace private. Around here, that wouldn't be easy.

After breakfast, Langer announced the voluntary interdenominational worship service, to which devout atheist Howard Andeker let out an enormous belch. "You're excused," Maury told him. "Anybody else want to leave?"

"Me," I said. If I was going to pray to anybody, it'd have to be the God of Food, and I was pretty sure his personal line to Camp Thin-na-Yet had been disconnected.

"All right," Maury said. "You guys hang around outside till we're through."

It was a beautiful day. Blue skies, puffy clouds, shafts of sunlight streaming through the trees. All the great things about the woods and countryside were out here, and all the rules and regulations and stupidities of camp were safely stowed away behind the mess-hall doors. I felt good for a change.

"Want to play some tetherball?" Andeker asked.

"No," I said irritably. Not only was Howard spoiling the natural beauty around me, he was also keeping me from reading Belinda's note.

"You sure?" he pressed.

"Yeah." Andeker was a demon at tetherball, mostly because he was the tallest kid in the cabin.

"Prayer services!" he snorted. "That stuff always amazes me!"

"People get brainwashed," I said.

"*We* didn't fall for it."

"That's because we have exceptionally dirty brains. Me, I've got ring-around-the-cerebellum."

"Hey, wait up!" somebody yelled. We turned around. Ambling toward us was none other than Franklin D. Schwartz.

"Frank! You okay?" I asked.

"I guess so. Did I miss anything?"

"Last night at the dance they gave everybody a free case of Almond Joys," Andeker said.

Frank laughed sadly. "That'll be the day."

"What was wrong with you?" I asked.

"They never figured it out. I guess I just fainted, period."

"Want to play tetherball?" Andeker asked.

"I better go to worship," Frank said, leaving Howard and me outside to solve the problems of the world.

When we got back to the cabin, Nick was looking awfully smug. Julius and I prepared ourselves for battle. Considering Nick's marvelous imagination, we figured he'd do something really original like sticking a frog or a snake or something equally obnoxious in our beds to get back at us for his undeserved punishment.

Nick's eyes followed us as we checked out our beds and our drawers. Nothing jumped or wriggled out at us, so we figured we were safe. I was dying to read Belinda's note, so I grabbed a comic book to hide it in and jumped up to my bunk.

The next thing I heard was a horrible metallic squeak. The springs and mattress caved in. I fell with them through the bedframe and onto Julius's head. Then his bunk gave way, and the two of us crashed to the floor. Fortunately that held up, or we'd've been dumped underneath the cabin with the rats and squirrels.

Everybody else thought it was the funniest thing they'd ever seen. Especially Nick.

Julius and I weren't exactly amused. We were really shaken up. But I didn't seem to be hurt beyond a couple of bruises. "Barris, I'll kill you!" Julius boomed as he untangled himself from the springs (tangling me worse in the process), so I knew he wasn't badly hurt, either.

Nick laughed even harder. I finally got free and rushed toward him, but he was outside and down the steps before I could get close. I gave up.

Not Julius. Bellowing like a mad bull, he lit out after Nick. The rest of us watched from the porch. Nick hid behind the latrines and kept popping out from one side and then the other. Panting, Julius finally had to come back to the cabin. For a minute he hovered over Nick's bunk as if he were trying to think of some perfect way of getting even, but then all he did was sit down and catch his breath. And rub the side of his head where the springs had caught him.

"What's going on up there?" Maury yelled from outside.

"Some of us are having trouble making our beds," Duff hollered.

Maury came in to have a look. A smile spread over his face. "How'd it happen?"

"Beats me," Julius said. He wasn't about to squeal on Nick.

Maury cracked up. It was the first time I'd seen

him really let himself go and laugh since camp started. He didn't seem the laughing type; maybe some sociology expert told him it wasn't professional to laugh. But now he just couldn't stop. "Toilet duty!" he finally announced, still shaking with laughter.

The one mistake Maury made was assigning Julius one of the mops. Julius wasn't too happy about it at first, but then he discovered he wouldn't have to bend down and get his hands dirty. He also found he could dip the mop in the toilet, sneak up on Nick outside, and flop the drippy end all over his head. Which, of course, he did. Nick tried to get back at him, but a mop is a pretty good defensive weapon.

So Maury had to declare a truce, which meant Nick and Julius had to shake hands and promise not to fight any more unless they wanted to be shipped off to the younger kids' cabins. You had to give these people credit for knowing their psychology, all right. Getting stuck in a cabin with a bunch of ten-year-olds would be just about the worst thing that could happen to you. Not only would you have to put up with the little kids, but you'd also have to endure taunts like "How many times did you flunk first grade?" and "Aren't you a little big for your age?" from the kids in your own cabin. So Nick and Julius were on their best behavior. At least for a while.

Belinda's note was still in my pocket, so when everybody else headed back to the cabin to change into swimsuits I stayed behind on my personally cleaned seat. Maybe I'm weird, but I've always considered the toilet to be the most private place there is. Usually nobody will come in and bother you. You can sit there as long as you want, and what you do is your own business.

Not at camp. The toilet stalls don't have locks. In fact, they don't even have doors. So nine times out of ten when you're sitting on the can, some jerk will come in and make some wisecrack about how often you go to the john or whatever, and this one, nice, leisurely, private pleasure turns into something you do in a big hurry because it's not private at all.

So as I sat there across from the sign that read, *"Be like dad, not like your date—Hoist the seat before you urinate,"* with the word "date" crossed out and the word "miss" written in above it, I half expected company, and I was pretty sneaky about unfolding Belinda's note.

It read:

> Must see you. Meet at 3 on path from crafts shed to mess hall under oak tree halfway down. Be there. Urgent.
>
> B.
>
> P.S.: Don't fail me.

Her handwriting was so flowery it almost smelled good, which made it hard for me to imagine what could be all that urgent. I wondered what she could possibly have in mind. I kept wondering so hard during swim class that I bumped my head into the

82

side of the pier and nearly drowned. I wondered so much during lunch that I accidentally drank from the diseased Frank Schwartz's glass of bug juice.

I'd've wondered my way through slimnastics, but the coach was working us double to make up for the fact that Frank was sitting it out because of his mysterious illness. So I was totally pooped by three, when it was time for either my first archery lesson or my meeting with Belinda.

I told Bernie and Howard not to wait for me to go to archery with them. Then I hid out for a while in the john. And I tried my best not to look like there was anything unusual about me as I walked up the path to the mess hall, which was the only way to get to my rendezvous without passing the archery field. I figured I'd be fine as long as I didn't run into somebody who knew where I was supposed to be.

Instead, I ran into Dr. Ira Langer himself, all decked out in shorts, sunglasses, and cigarette, with his tennis racket under his arm. "What's your hurry?" he asked cheerily. I tried to pretend I hadn't heard.

"Hey! Slow down a second!" he yelled, jogging up alongside me. I figured I'd better say something.

"I'm late for activity," I said.

"Which activity?" he asked, falling into step with me.

How was I going to lie my way out of this one? "Oh, uh, crafts."

"Headed that way myself," he said. "Let's walk together."

"Great," I said, sounding about as convincing as those announcers who pitch instant weight-loss pills on TV. Belinda was right: I had no talent for dishonesty.

But I did know exactly what Langer would say next. Not that I believe in ESP or anything, but I knew and he said it: "Well, what do you think of camp?"

"It's okay," I lied.

"How's your reducing program coming?"

"I've lost five pounds."

"How do you feel about that?"

"Five pounds lighter?"

"Truthfully, now. Isn't it a good feeling?"

Truthfully? Mostly it was a hungry feeling, and an empty one, a feeling of being leaned on. "Yeah, I guess."

"When you get home after camp, you'll be able to continue the habits you've developed here," Langer said. "We have a very impressive record of success."

"Oh, yeah?" I wanted to say. I wanted to ask him why people like Franklin Schwartz were back up here for second helpings of this place if the camp were really all that successful. What I actually did was sort of nod and say "Um."

I knew we were getting close to that oak, at least the one I thought Belinda meant, since three or four of them along the path more or less fit the description, but I didn't see any sign of her. Maybe she wasn't there, but if she was, I didn't want Langer to catch her just standing around doing nothing. Around here, that was a major crime. I was just about to ask him some dumb question—anything to keep the conversation going so that Belinda could hear us and duck out of sight—when he hit me with his surprise.

"You're in the red cabin, right?"

I nodded.

"What do you know about that incident in the counselors' cabin last night?"

My guilt grabbed me again. How much did he know about the break-in? Did he suspect me? Or Belinda? Probably not, but then . . . "Not much," I answered.

"What do you think about it?"

"What's to think?"

"I think it was a dumb stunt. Exceptionally childish." I could feel a knot tighten in my stomach the instant he got the words out. "If people have complaints, the adult thing for them to do is come see me. I'm always willing to listen," he said, testing his overhead smash.

"I have a complaint," I said.

"Shoot."

"Why don't you get more archery equipment?"

"What's wrong with what we've got?"

"There's not enough. The classes keep getting filled up."

"For one thing, archery's not exactly the most active sport," Langer said patiently. "We'd rather encourage you to do more strenuous things, like swimming or hiking or dancing."

"Crafts isn't very strenuous."

"It's not a sport, either," he said as we neared the crafts shed. "But tennis is, and I'm off to the court. Keep up the good work." He gave me a fatherly pat on the back and waited for me to go in.

I didn't have much choice, so I stepped through the door. "Hey, you're late!" Frank Schwartz yelled.

I hoped I could make the next scene look good. "Wait a minute!" I said, slapping myself on the forehead. "Today's Sunday, right?"

Christina, the crafts person, looked up at me from the potter's wheel. "All day," she said, smiling.

"I don't know how I could've goofed up," I said. "I'm scheduled for archery today."

"Are you sure?"

"Yeah. I've been waiting for it all week."

"Better hurry on over there before they run out of arrows." Christina was basically an okay person. If I hadn't been so totally spastic in art, I'd probably have hung around the crafts shed a lot. The nice thing about Christina was that she cared more about the kids and their problems than she did about enforcing dumb rules.

I rushed out the door and steamed straight up the path toward the oak tree. Considering I usually finished last in school races when I finished at all, I couldn't've really been moving that fast, but a minute later I heard a familiar voice call, "Hey, slow down, Speedy Gonzales!" Belinda, of course. I ran to the nearest oak, but I couldn't see her.

"Over here, Flash!" she cried, but trees were all I could find in the direction of her voice. "Hey, Daniel Boone!" she yelled, and stood up for a second. Then she stooped down again behind some tall ferns underneath a bunch of sapling branches some campers of yesteryear must've lashed together into a little shelter. I made my way over and stooped down beside her.

"God!" she said. "How'd you manage to pick up Dr. Strangler?"

"My native talent."

"Zimmer, something tells me you're even wimpier than you look."

"If you called me here just to insult me," I said, "I'll go shoot some arrows."

"Oh, come on. You remember my abrasive style."

"After Langer, I'm not in the mood for it."

"But it's part of my charm!"

"Look, what's the big mystery? I'm missing archery."

"Well, my word!" Belinda hooted. "What a sacrifice!"

"If you knew how hard it is to get into that class, you wouldn't act so snotty. Come on, what's up?"

"What if I told you I was pregnant?"

Now, I know you can't get pregnant from kissing, and even if you could, you wouldn't know about it overnight, but it certainly wasn't a question I was prepared for. I just stood there and gave her a funny stare.

She laughed. "Just wanted to see how you'd react."

"Very funny. I'm going to archery class." I turned away.

Belinda grabbed my arm. "Oh, hold on. I don't mean to be weird. What happened last night?"

"You were there."

"I mean after."

"Not much. Julius hid his stuff in another guy's footlocker—Nick, the creep, you remember—and my counselor found it. Nick's getting extra exercises and no canteen for a week. Is that what was so urgent?"

"No. I want to know if you want to help me break out."

Another surprise. "What?" I said.

"You know you'd like to get out of here. Admit it."

"I'd like to be rich and famous, too."

"We could leave with hardly any trouble at all. Wouldn't you love to run wild in a supermarket? Or a McDonald's?"

"Belinda, I'm stuck up here for five more weeks. Don't make my life miserable by teasing me."

"I'm not kidding. It'd be fantastic."

"We'd get caught."

"Then they'd have no choice but to send us home. I mean, they couldn't have us running wild among the other campers, could they?"

"They could lock us in the infirmary and dose us with sleeping pills till camp was over," I said.

"You've been watching too many TV shows."

"Look, Belinda, I figure it this way. As long as I'm here, I may as well make it easy on myself. Who knows? I might even get thin."

"You'll just gain it all back again the minute you hit the real world."

"Maybe not."

"Ha! You know what's out there? Calories! And you don't have the willpower to resist them. One-pound bags of potato chips will jump out at you from the shelves, crying, 'Eat me!' Candy bars will attack you from vending machines. Ice cream cones will seduce you. You'll order doubles, then triples, then banana splits, and before you know it, you'll be eating half gallons straight from the box." She made it sound so real I half expected a carton of butter pecan to materialize on the spot.

"How is running away going to help?" I demanded.

"At least it'll prove you have an iota or two of self-respect, which is what we fat people aren't supposed to have any of, which is why we don't care what we look like, which is why we stuff our faces. So we come up to this place, and they won't let us have enough self-respect to blow our own noses. We're supposed to act like zombies and lose weight for the simple reason there's no choice about it."

"Look, I don't like this place any better than you do, but I don't see what good it'd do just to run off for a day or two."

"It'd be a protest. A symbol."

"If you want to protest, why not get up a petition?"

"That's a good one!" Belinda snorted. "Langer would have the biggest laugh in history. What would the petition say? 'We, the slobs of Camp Thin-na-Yet, in order to establish quieter stomachs, do hereby demand that more food should cross our lips'? Don't be stupid. It wouldn't work. Langer would just crack down on the troublemakers."

"We could call a strike."

"Zimmer, where's your brain? We're not working for them. What are we going to refuse to do?"

"I don't know. Go to slimnastics?"

"That's about as sensible as a hunger strike! Besides, most of the kids here are too chicken-livered even to offend their counselors. Some of them haven't ever been away from home before, and people have laughed at them for so long they can't even take themselves seriously. If we want to protest, we'll have to do it on our own. I say, let's run away."

"I don't want to."

"You're spineless."

"At least I'm not an imbecile."

Belinda squeezed my hand. "Come on. I can't do this alone."

"No. Count me out."

She let go of my hand. "Okay, Captain Courageous. See you around." She clomped out through the underbrush and headed down the path.

I felt rotten. First I'd missed my archery lesson, and now I'd lost a friend, the one girl in the entire universe who'd ever been halfway nice to me, unless you counted this classmate of mine in the first grade who had a crush on me because I knew how to print her name and she didn't.

And I really liked Belinda. She really had guts. All I could see ahead of me was five dismal weeks of heat and starvation and regimentation and gloom, but the prospect of running away and getting caught and punished sounded even gloomier. Yet Belinda looked right past all that gloom to freedom. And a square meal. In that sense I had to admit her idea sounded very appealing.

But it also sounded even stupider than our little burglary party. It reminded me of those comic strips where a little kid wraps up all his candy bars in his polka-dot hankie and ties it to a stick hobo-style and runs away from home. Only worse. We didn't even have the candy bars. I could just see the headlines in the local paper: FAT CAMPERS SAVED FROM STARVATION IN WOODS; PUT BACK ON DIET.

As I tramped past the mess hall, I noticed the night's schedule: "All Camp Activity—New Games—Socker Field." Whoever was in charge of this sign must've skipped spelling—the other day, it said "Warship Services"—but I got the idea. One gym coach I had in school was a big believer in these "New Games," noncompetitive things like "Everybody Jump Up and Down" or "Follow the Guy in Front of You" where you're supposed to have a lot of fun because there's no such thing as winning them.

But I was so down right then that an awful thought crossed my mind: the way things were going, I just might become the first person in the history of "New Games" ever to lose one.

12

The counselors must've been reading my mind. Next morning, they divided us up on the lawn for group therapy. Just what I needed.

Miss Shirt came over to my circle to lead our group. She was wearing glasses. I guess she thought it made her look intellectual. "Okay," she said, after taking a very serious look at her clipboard. "I want you all to talk about how you see yourselves. Who wants to go first?"

All the girls raised their hands. "Carol?"

Carol beamed, then frowned. "I'm short and fat and unattractive, and I don't think anybody cares about me."

Shirt thanked her and called on Ellen. "I'm fat and ugly and nobody cares about me at all. And my eyebrows are too thick."

Nick Barris dug an elbow into my ribs and smirked. Shirt jotted something down on her clipboard. "Fine. Doreen?"

"I'm short and fat and ugly, too, and nobody gives a damn about me, either. And my teeth are crooked, and my nose is too big." It reminded me of "The House That Jack Built."

Shirt pointed at me. I said, "I'm tall and thin and handsome, and girls whistle at me when I walk by."

Shirt scowled. "Really? That's really how you see yourself?"

I grinned. "Yeah."

"I don't think you're so handsome," Ellen said.

"Well, I don't think your eyebrows are all that thick," I shot back. This whole thing was so idiotic, the only way I could treat it was as a joke.

"Come on," Shirt urged me. "How do you really see yourself?"

"How do *you* see yourself?" I asked.

"I'm the leader of this group. I'm not the one with a problem."

"In other words, you're perfect," I said.

I could see her starting to redden. "This session is for your benefit, not mine. How I feel about myself is irrelevant. Now, who's next?"

A guy from the blue cabin raised his hand. "All right," Shirt said. "How do you see yourself?"

"With a mirror."

"A wide-angle one, I'll bet," Nick put in. "And me, I'm Popeye, The Sailor Man, toot-toot!"

"Look, gang, how about a little cooperation?" Shirt pleaded. "This isn't a joke session."

"Why did the fireman wear red suspenders?" piped the guy from the blue cabin.

Nick and I answered at the same time: "To keep his pants up."

Shirt was furious. "One more crack out of you boys, and you go see Dr. Langer."

94

Twenty-four knuckles cracked at once. Shirt threw her pencil at me and yelled, "You three! Out! Right now! You tell Dr. Langer I sent you!"

Langer was leading his own group at the other end of the lawn. In the middle of listening to some guy whine about how insecure he was, the great doctor looked up and noticed me and Nick and the other kid. "Problem?" he asked, taking a pull on his cigarette. "I've got a group here."

"She sent us over," I said, pointing.

"Why?"

I shrugged. So did Nick and the other guy.

"Sit down," Langer said. "We'll discuss that later."

I sat down next to Belinda. She frowned at me as Langer started in again. "Okay. People start eating because they're insecure, and then they get fat, which makes them even more insecure, so they keep on eating and get even fatter. It's a vicious circle. What if you said to yourself, 'I'm not going to gain any more weight. I'm going to feel proud whenever I lose a pound, whenever I pass up dessert.' "

"What?" Belinda cried. "Up here there's no dessert to pass up. There's no choice about whether we lose weight or not. How are we supposed to feel proud about it?"

"Let me ask you something. What if I went out and got a big piece of pie and set it in front of you right now? Would you eat it?"

"You bet!" Belinda said.

"Right. Okay. That's exactly why we're not giving you the choice. Once you start modifying your behavior, then you'll be able to make the right decisions for yourself."

Belinda snorted. "Why don't you just sew our mouths shut and feed us intravenously?"

"What's your name?" Langer asked, annoyed.

"Belinda Moss."

"Belinda, let me tell you something. I've had ten years of experience as a clinical psychologist. I've seen all kinds of people over the years. You know what their biggest problem is?"

"I can't guess," Belinda said.

"Hostility. Hostility like yours. It's exactly that kind of hostility that's causing your problems, and don't tell me you don't have problems, because anybody who just walks past you can see them. Now, we're here trying to make an honest effort to help you, and you're just closing your mind and being hostile and refusing to let us help. And that's the kind of attitude you're going to have to change before I or anybody else can be any help to you at all."

Langer took a long drag on his cigarette and nonchalantly exhaled a big smoke cloud in a way that let you know he'd've blown smoke letters that spelled out "I'm the expert" if he knew how. Everybody waited to see what he'd say next. "If you want to stay exactly as you are and disappoint your parents and yourself for the rest of your life, fine. Nobody said it'd be easy to change your attitude or your habits. But until you do, you're going to be as miserable as you are right now."

You could see it hit Belinda hard, being singled

96

out in front of everybody as miserable. A loser. A failure. A failure among failures. Her lower lip quivered as if she might start crying any second. But as I said, Belinda had guts.

"You're not exactly flawless yourself," she told Langer. "You sit there telling us to break our bad habits, and the whole time you're sucking on those cigarettes the way babies suck on pacifiers. Okay, maybe I do have a pimply face and a rotten figure because of my insecurities. But I wouldn't like to see an X ray of your lungs."

Cool as a popsicle, Langer took another puff of his cigarette. He did it defiantly, the way you do when somebody tells you you're eating too much and you eat more just to prove you won't let anybody boss you around. "Finished?"

"Yeah," Belinda said, standing up. "And I'm not sticking around here to be insulted. If the rest of you could find your backbones, you wouldn't either." She stared at me, but I was too confused to move. It wasn't that I didn't agree with everything she'd said, but I'd already been kicked out of one group this morning, which would probably mean trouble enough in itself. Also, I kind of wanted to see how Langer would handle this. So I stayed put.

Belinda's stare turned nasty. She strode off across the lawn. "We can't work magic," Langer told the rest of us. "We can't help you if you won't try to help yourself. She's a very frustrated individual."

Right now she was, for sure. She was probably running through the woods, crying or trying hard

97

not to. I wondered whether it'd be better for me to find her and tell her what a nincompoop I thought Langer was, or just let her alone. I couldn't decide.

"Okay," Langer said. "Let's look at this from another angle. What makes you feel good about yourself?"

"When I finish something that was hard to do," said a girl who was trying for the Miss Suckup award.

"Sure! When you have a goal and you achieve it, you do feel good. Now, what kind of goals could we set for ourselves?"

Suddenly Langer reminded me of this awful guy who used to be on a TV show for kids. His name was Safari Sam, and he always said, "Now, boys and girls, what do we always do before we cross the street?" and stuff like that. Langer was smoother, but almost as condescending, and his effect on me was the same. I switched him off.

And got up and walked away.

"Where do you think you're going?" he yelled.

I just kept walking.

"Come back here!" he commanded. I thought he'd either get up and come after me or yell that I'd have to skip lunch today, but somehow I didn't care. I kept on walking.

"Zimmer, you get back here!" he yelled. I pretended I was deaf. And dumb, because I knew if I opened my mouth, I might tell Langer about a brand new habit I was trying to form: avoiding him.

13

As I stepped into the woods, I half expected Langer to send somebody after me, but it didn't happen. He was probably too busy explaining to the others what an insecure little blubberbutt I was.

I found Belinda in her special place under those bent saplings. She was sobbing. At first I wasn't quite sure whether I ought to intrude on her, but then something told me I ought to. I walked up to her.

Her face was buried in her hands, but I knew she could hear me coming. She kept on crying. She didn't say a word.

"Hey, calm down," I said softly. "You were right."

Belinda looked at me through her fingers. "No, he is. I *am* too hostile," she said through her tears.

"He's an idiot," I said. "There's a difference between just being hostile in general and being hostile about something you have every right to be hostile about. Like the way they treat us up here."

"But it works. Everybody's losing weight. Even me."

"Come on. Don't tell me *you're* getting sucked in by their propaganda."

"I don't know," she sobbed. "I'm all mixed up."

"Me, too. I'd like to be thin, but it's not worth going to prison to do it. It's means and ends."

"Huh?" Belinda took her hands down from her face and scowled at me.

"I had a teacher a couple years ago who was big on ethics. She used to show us examples of how you could have noble goals and how wrong it would be if you had to do rotten things to achieve them. Like, it'd be nice if all the buses and trains ran on time, but if it meant you had to have a dictatorship to do it, you'd probably decide it wasn't so bad to have the bus run late once in a while. Means and ends, see?"

Belinda frowned. "I know what means and ends are, Plato. I thought you said 'beans' and something. God, you can see where my mind's at."

"See? You're feeling better already."

Belinda was wiping her face on the sleeve of her T-shirt. I kissed some salty tears from her cheek. "Hey," I said. "Don't let those toothpicks brainwash you. You're a person, same as they are."

She smiled. "Only more so."

"Only more so."

Belinda brushed her hair from her moist gray eyes. "Now what?"

"Boy, I don't know. Langer was really pissed off at me for taking off from his wonderful group session without giving him any idea why."

"What do you think he'll do?"

"Make me skip lunch or something. I'll live."

"Let's run away. Right now."

"What would that solve? Maybe we should just write our parents that we've had enough. Ask them to come and get us."

"Oh, sure. I know what mine would say: 'Dear Daughter: Sometimes you can't always do just what you want. We're sure this camp will be good experience for you in learning how to cope with problems in your life. Et cetera, et cetera, blah, blah, blah. Love, Mom and Dad.' "

She had a point. We talked about parents for a while, and we talked about life in general, and then a girl's voice yelled from the path. "Hey, is that you in there?"

"Aw, hell," Belinda said to me. "No, the boogie man!" she hollered.

"Is that you, Belinda?" the girl yelled back.

"Give me a break, huh, Marcie?" Belinda pleaded.

"I ran ahead. The rest of the cabin'll be down in a second."

"Hang on!" Belinda shouted. She sighed and turned to me. "No sense being late for the swimsuit competition. See you later, Zimmer. Thanks." She squeezed my hand, gave me a peck on the nose, and tramped through the ferns to meet her cabinmate.

"Was that some guy in there with you?" Marcie wanted to know.

"Now, who would possibly be in there with me?" Belinda said.

"That guy who came to our group with those

other two. You know, from the dance. He left the group right after you did."

"Don't be ridiculous," Belinda said. I might've felt insulted if I hadn't realized I'd've said the exact same thing in her place. Camp was tough enough without having your cabinmates get on you about your "lover."

"I just thought maybe," Marcie said. "Boy, I couldn't believe what you said to Dr. Langer. I'd never say anything like that in a million years."

"Well, you're not a quivering mass of hostility like me," Belinda snorted. Then the rest of the cabin caught up with them and drowned them out in a sea of girl-noise.

I wasn't in the mood to meet up with Langer just yet, so I took the long way back to the cabin. Everybody was getting ready for slimnastics when I walked in the door.

"You're in luck," Julius said. "You don't have to hit slimnastics today."

"You get to do deep knee bends with Langer instead," Andeker informed me.

"The knight in shining armor," Nick laughed. "Defending his lady love."

"What a load of crap," I said.

"She certainly looks like one," said Nick.

"You go to hell," I snapped.

"Your mother didn't leave the door open."

I ignored him. Right now, the last thing I needed was two-hundred-odd pounds of Nick Barris on top of me. "What's the story?" I asked Julius. "Am I supposed to go see Langer, or what?"

"Yup. He said he wanted to see you in his office the minute you showed up."

"Great," I said, stalking out the door. "Wonderful."

Walking up the path, I got the kind of feeling that in all those medieval fantasies I used to read they always called "nameless dread." Usually the person who got the feeling was a hero who was up against some evil wizard with vast powers who might zap him with some sort of magical ray or web or spell if he wasn't careful.

I was no hero, but I had the feeling I was about to be zapped. Langer was about as magical as a packet of Kool-Aid, but he definitely had unknown powers. As I plodded up the trail, I felt I was about to confront a mortal foe. I hadn't had much experience with psychologists. There was no telling what one might do. Deliver a hard punch to your ego, maybe, or kick you in the soul.

"Come in," Langer said when I knocked on his door. I did. The air conditioning felt good. Maybe this wouldn't be so terrible after all. Maybe he'd admire me for my guts. "Sit down," Langer said. I sat.

Langer's first move was to say nothing. He just sat there in his shorts and Camp Thin-na-Yet T-shirt and rocked back and forth in his swivel chair with his fingers interlocked behind his neck. He wasn't smoking, probably because he didn't want me to be able to use that against him. He just sat and rocked and glared at me once in a while.

If there's anything that'll make you feel uncomfortable, it's being stared at by somebody who rocks back and forth in front of you and doesn't say anything. At least when somebody's yelling at you, sooner or later you have a chance to yell back. But somehow, shutting up isn't very satisfying. You start thinking about what your hands are doing and whether you should scratch your head or not, because in the midst of all this silence, everything seems magnified. After a while, I'd finally had enough. I was all ready to tell Langer to quit wasting my time and get to the point when he let out an enormous sigh. "What am I going to do about you, Sam?" he asked wearily.

"I give up."

Langer swiveled up to the desk and stared at me. This meant he was going to get very serious. "Sam, everything I read in your folder tells me what a bright person you are. You get good grades, you don't seem to have any major problems. So what I want to know is, where did you pick up all this hostility?"

That word again. "Right here at camp," I said. "It's the only place I've ever been treated like a convict."

"A convict?"

"Yeah. Except convicts get three square meals a day."

"That's all you can think about, isn't it?" Langer's voice dripped with contempt.

"Not really. I also think about how I don't have any freedom to do what I want to. If I want to listen to the radio after nine o'clock, there's some dumb rule that says I can't. If I want to read a book instead of going swimming, there's a rule that says I'm not allowed to. If I want to shoot a bow and arrow, there's a rule that says I have to take crafts instead."

"All societies have rules, Sam. They're for your own good."

"I'll bet that's what prison wardens say."

Langer turned sarcastic. "You're really having a terrible time here, aren't you? No fun at all."

"Right."

"Tell you what. Why don't you pick up the phone right this minute and tell your parents exactly what you told me?"

At first the idea sounded so good I nearly grabbed for the receiver. Then I started thinking, and I held back. Sometimes I think too much.

Number one, if I told my parents my troubles, they certainly weren't going to be able to get Langer to change the food and the rules and the archery schedules and the people. There wasn't a thing they could do about any of it. So in the end I'd have to ask them to let me come home. Which, as Belinda pointed out, they probably wouldn't even consider. Something about facing up to my responsibilities.

But if by some chance I managed to convince

them to come and get me, they'd be furious for weeks. Langer certainly wouldn't give them their money back, and they'd be mad about that. They'd probably have to change their plans for their trip to Europe, and they'd be mad about that. And they'd just be mad at me in general, for being a quitter and letting them down. If I went home, I'd be doomed to a summer of hearing how disappointed my parents were in me.

"Well?" Langer said, handing me the phone.

"They'd be at work now," I said, stalling. "They don't like me to call them unless it's an emergency."

"I thought this was an emergency. You can't stand it here another minute. Go ahead. Say whatever you like. I'll go outside if that's what's bothering you." Langer kept holding the phone at the end of his outstretched arm, thrusting it at me. For some reason it seemed enormous, threatening. I couldn't handle it.

"I don't want to call them," I said finally.

"You sure?"

I nodded.

Langer put the phone back on his desk. "You're not the first person who's ever gotten homesick. But now you've had your chance to complain to the people who've sent you here. You've chosen not to. So things can't be all that bad."

"I didn't say that."

"I'm saying it. Your problems are mostly up here." He pointed to his head. "You'll get them straightened out, I'm sure. But from now on, how about taking your hostilities out on the tetherball or something?"

I didn't say anything. I knew I wouldn't be able to pinpoint it till I went back and thought it over, but I knew the sorcerer had somehow gotten the better of me. He'd worked some kind of spell, and I was powerless to resist. Or maybe I'd worked the spell on myself. The only consolation I could think of was that sometimes even in the old tales the wizards best the heroes temporarily. Though a hero was the furthest thing from what I felt like.

"Okay, Sam. I think you see what I'm saying. You can go back to your cabin."

I was in a trance. I got up to leave. As I went through the door, Langer's voice came after me. In the calmest tones imaginable, it said, "By the way, you'll have to skip lunch today."

I pushed the door hard behind me. Instead of slamming, it just squooshed. It had one of those pneumatic closers on it. There is nothing more frustrating than slamming a door and having it go squoosh.

I had tears in my eyes as I went over to the tetherball and punched it as hard as I could. It whirled around the pole and smacked me in the neck.

14

At the lunch I missed, Langer announced the week's big deal, the one you had to meet the weight goal to get. It was a camping trip. Actually, the camping trip was only for the older guys' cabins. The girls and little kids would get to see a movie. So luck was with me for a change. I had seen that movie two years before, and it stank.

I always liked campouts. On this one we'd even get to canoe across the lake. But what I couldn't imagine was a camping trip without the most important thing of all, namely tons of food. Two years ago I'd eaten ten hot dogs on one cookout, and I could easily have stuffed down more, but they ran out. This year? We consulted Frank Schwartz.

"Hot dogs are fattening," he informed us.

"What do you eat, then?" Julius asked. "Fried cattails?"

"Last year we got hamburgers," Frank said.

Everybody perked up a little. "How many?" Russ Duff asked suspiciously.

"One each," Frank said. Everybody perked down again.

"What else?" Andeker asked.

"An ear of roasted corn. A potato. Two pats of butter and a lot of vegetables. Of course, it might be different this year," Frank said optimistically.

"Toasted marshmallows?" I asked him.

"Sure," Frank said. "We got ten apiece."

"Well, hallelujah!" Nick said, brightening.

"Low-cal marshmallows," Frank continued gloomily. "They taste like pillow stuffing."

"When do we start?" Nick groaned.

I wanted to groan, too. But there were at least two points in the campout's favor: it would be a welcome change from the routine around here, and they probably wouldn't bring the slimnastics coach along.

But on Tuesday morning, my weight was exactly the same as the day before. Not the usual half-pound under. Not even a quarter-pound. The same. It happened again on Wednesday. I couldn't figure it out.

On Thursday, I was one pound up. "That's impossible," I said. "I haven't been eating anything. I even missed lunch on Monday."

"It happens sometimes," Maury said. "Don't let it throw you."

"Great," I said, trying to hide how upset I was. After Maury left, I went to the toilet. A minute or so later, Frank Schwartz sat down in the other stall.

"Now you know why I put those rocks in my pockets," he said.

"I don't get it," I said. "How could I gain weight when I'm not eating anything?"

"You hit the wall."

"Huh?"

"It happens to everybody sooner or later. The thinner you are to start with, the sooner it happens."

"How come?"

"The first weight you lose is mostly water. That comes off quick. Then you hit real fat, which is a lot harder to lose."

"But how can you gain weight when you're not eating enough for a flea?"

"All sorts of ways. Your body weighs more on humid days than on dry ones. Or you ate saltier food yesterday and your body retained more water. I read about all this after I got home last year. They won't tell you anything about it here, because they think the less you know, the harder you'll work. I got gypped out of my first camping trip last year because of it."

"Isn't there anything you can do? I need to drop those two pounds to make the trip."

"I tried praying."

"Did it work?"

"You kidding?"

It looked pretty bad, all right. At the lunchtime weight roundup, I got one of Miss Shirt's patented tsk-tsks for actually gaining. Belinda gave me a look as though she couldn't believe it. I just sort of shrugged. Afterwards, I asked Maury what would happen if I didn't lose those two pounds by tomorrow morning.

"Maybe you will. Think thin."

"I'm thinking thin. But what if?"

"You've been doing fine so far. Keep it up."
He walked away. It was crystal clear that if I didn't lose those pounds, I could forget about the camping trip.

I started thinking about all the quick weight-loss tricks I'd ever heard of. Maybe I could vomit my lunch. I once knew a kid who said his cousin could make himself barf by sticking his fingers down his throat. But just the idea of that made me nauseous, so I ruled it out.

I could cut my hair, but it wasn't all that long yet anyway. Besides, I always looked dumb with short hair, and it probably wouldn't amount to much on the scale. So much for goofy ideas.

One thing I actually could do would be to skip dinner. That ought to help. And I could avoid drinking water the rest of the day. If I kept active, moved around a lot, maybe, just maybe, I could knock off those two ridiculous pounds by morning. Just the thought of a real grilled hamburger, just one juicy hunk of meat, instead of those wafer-thin precooked burgers with imitation grill marks painted on that they served at mess hall—that alone would be worth the effort. The marshmallows wouldn't hurt, either.

Even though it was ninety degrees in the shade and I was thirsty, I passed right by the water fountain. Walking uses up more calories than sitting, so during active rest I paced back and forth while I reread some of my favorite Uncle Scrooge comics. It drove everybody crazy.

"Sit down, Zimmer. It's like watching a robot," Andeker said.

"It's hopeless anyway," Duff insisted. "You won't lose two pounds by tomorrow."

I kept on walking. They'd annoyed me plenty of times, and damn it, I wanted to go on that campout.

I was just about dying of thirst when we hit the field for slimnastics, but I'd vowed I wasn't going to take a drink the rest of the day, so I just suffered. As I stood at attention in the withering heat and listened to Coach Dallesandro explain for the umpteenth time the principles of slimnastics and the benefits of exercise, I tried not to think about how thirsty I was. But about halfway through our second set of jumping-jacks, I started to bark and wheeze.

"What's the MATter?" the coach hollered at me in that way gym teachers have of making their sentences get louder in the middle. I just kept jumping and panting and rasping until it was time for sit-ups, which I got through okay somehow.

Then it was back to jumping jacks. Dallesandro was hollering "Let's MOVE!" when suddenly I made a noise that sounded like "Bluh!" or "Blah!" or "Bleh!" and fell on my face. Everybody stopped to look. I could see them. I just couldn't move.

"Come on, guys, keep it UP! Let's GO! FIF-teen! SIX-teen! HIGH-er! HIGH-er!" Dallesandro yelled as he walked over to me. "Hey, pal, what's the trouble?" he asked, but when I moved my lips to tell him, nothing came out. Then everybody went dark, and I heard some hollering and somebody who said "Faking it," and the next thing I knew I woke up in a bed where a prune-faced woman in white was taking a thermometer out of my mouth.

"Where am I?" I asked. I know this sounds like the kind of dumb question you only hear in the movies after some guy's been clobbered by the villain, but that's really what I said, all right: "Where am I?"

"The infirmary," she said. "You fainted. The heat must've been too much for you."

I should've guessed. "Can I have some water?"

She picked up a pitcher and poured me a glassful, then stuck one of those flexible straws in it so I could drink without having to sit up very far. The water was warm and tasted like a swamp. "How about some ice?" I asked.

"You don't want anything cold just yet. Sip it slowly."

I looked around while I sipped. Not much to look at. Basically, it was just a big room with a couple of cots and a medicine cabinet and some tongue depressors and a stethoscope lying around. It smelled like disinfectant. "Are you a nurse?" I asked the woman, who was busy writing something on a clipboard. Everybody had clipboards at this camp. If something happened to the clipboard industry, Camp Thin-na-Yet would be ruined. "Are you a nurse?" I asked again.

"I'm in charge of the infirmary," she said, which meant she wasn't a nurse. If she were a nurse, she'd be proud to say so. Langer undoubtedly figured he could save a few extra bucks by hiring this untrained wonder to run the infirmary.

"Is there a doctor around?" I asked. Swampy or not, the water was perking me up.

"Drink some more," she said. "You're probably dehydrated."

Then I remembered why I'd fainted, and I felt like a first-class idiot. Here I was in the infirmary just because I was willing to risk my health—my life, maybe—to go on some dumb camping trip. Pretty stupid, all right. I took another sip of water and sat up.

"How do you feel?" the woman asked.

"A little dizzy."

"Lie down. You don't want to faint again."

"I think I'll be okay."

"Lie down and let us decide that, please."

I lay back and humored her. I didn't feel all that terrific, but I really didn't want to spend the rest of the day in the infirmary. Next thing I knew, I was waking up. It was almost six o'clock.

"Feeling any better?" Madame Infirmary asked.

"Yeah," I said. "I'm hungry."

"I wouldn't be a bit surprised."

I swung my legs over the side of the bed. I felt okay. "I think I'm all right. Can I go to supper?"

"Are you sure you're well enough?"

I walked around a little. "Yeah. I'm okay."

"Then you'd better get over to the mess hall. If you feel faint again, be sure and tell your counselor."

I put on my shoes and headed for the mess hall. The rest of my cabin was coming up the path. "Hey! Zimmer! You okay?" Duff shouted.

"Yeah. I think so," I said.

"He's just allergic to exercise," Andeker sniffed.

"Seriously, you okay?" Julius asked, concerned.

"Yeah, I guess. They said I fainted."

"Did you ever! The coach looked like he'd faint too when he saw what happened."

We all went into the mess hall. "What a stupid thing to do," Frank Schwartz told me.

"Yeah, I fainted on purpose. Do it all the time. I'm the Mad Fainter," I said.

"Not fainting. Leaving the infirmary before dinner. If you'd stayed, you'd've gotten some real food. If you have to spend time in that place, you may as well get something out of it."

A foot in my head kicked me. What a day. Still, I played extra hard at capture-the-flag that evening on the rec field in the hope I could still make the weight goal. But after about ten minutes of running around, I suddenly felt almost as rotten as I had when I woke up in the infirmary, and I had to slow down. The campout was lost. No doubt about it.

As I lay in bed that night, all I could think of were those two extra pounds. Two pounds that would keep me from the trip. Two pounds that appeared magically from out of nowhere only because I wasn't totally gross to begin with. It wasn't fair. I'd said that a lot in my lifetime, but this time it was for real. It wasn't as if I'd been sneaking Mr. Goodbars or something. I'd been cooperating in my weight-loss program. What did these jerks want from me?

The solution came to me in a dream. I chopped off my right hand and plunked it, all dripping and bloody, on Langer's desk. "Here's your two pounds of flesh!" I screamed. The worst part of the dream was that Langer actually looked pleased and said something about how proud he was of me.

I woke up. I'd been lying on my arm, and it was all numb and needly. I woke Julius up trying to pound it back to life.

The next morning at weigh-in, I went last. Maybe I'd lose an ounce or two just standing around. I also left off my socks and underpants. No sense not giving everything a try. But when I stepped on the scale, I was exactly one pound over my weight goal for the week. Maybe just three-quarters of a pound, actually. It might as well have been a ton.

"Are you sure you're reading that right?" I asked.

"You blew it, champ," Maury said.

I stepped off and on again. "Check it one more time."

"Exactly the same. You're out of luck. You guys get ready for breakfast." He picked up the scale and walked out the door.

I followed him. "Couldn't you fudge it? I could make it up next week."

"Why would I want to do that?"

"To be nice."

"Zimmer, we have rules. I'm doing what's best for you. You'll have other chances to go on overnights."

"It's not fair. My parents paid for me to go on campouts."

"They also paid for you to lose weight."

"But I'm losing weight. Hell, it's only one lousy pound."

"Every lousy pound counts." Maury walked away. No question, I was out of luck. Back inside, my charming cabinmates gave me a lot of heartfelt "Too bads" and "Sorrys" and "It's a shames." Nothing like sympathy to cheer you up.

At lunch they crowned the week's queen and king of weight loss, who turned out to be the same enormous girl as last week and—wonder of wonders—Julius. Like last time, the girl wore this terribly embarrassed smile, as if she knew the only reason she was up there was her horrendously gluttonous past.

But with Julius it was different. You could tell it was the first time he'd ever won anything, or at least anything that involved a ceremony, and he was all bashful and awkward and modest and proud. It would be something he could write home and tell his dad about, and it was touching in a dumb sort of way. I felt good for him.

But then Miss Shirt started reading off the weekly weight-loss totals, with little squeals of delight for the kids who did well and little frowny scolds for the kids who screwed up, and I had to try to act nonchalant when she got to me. "Last, and I'm afraid, least, in the red cabin, Sam Zimmer, three pounds lost. Oh, come on, Sam. You can do better than that. Next week, I want to see *you* win that crown." Julius sort of half smiled when she said that.

I looked toward Belinda. She winced and shook her head. I couldn't tell whether she was sympathetic or disgusted. I certainly was disgusted.

After slimnastics, we spent the rest of the afternoon getting our sleeping bags and canteens and mess kits and insect repellents together for the big campout. All but one of us. I wished they'd leave already and give me some peace and quiet.

Then Maury stuck his head in the door and asked to see me outside for a second. I jumped down from the bunk and hurried out to the porch. And I do mean hurried. Maybe he felt sorry for me or something and had changed his mind about letting me come along.

"What's up?" I asked.

"Pack up some of your clothes and your toothbrush and soap and things. Enough to tide you over till we get back."

"Huh?"

"There won't be anybody down here while we're away. You're going to bunk with the green-stripers."

"You've got to be kidding!" I screamed. "That's little kids! I'm not staying with little kids!"

"All the older guys are going on the campout. It's only for a couple of days."

118

"I won't do it."

"I'm not going to stand here and argue with you."

"I'll manage fine right here. I don't need anybody to wipe my nose."

"I'm not gonna tell you again, Zimmer. Pack up."

Democracy, it's wonderful.

Once Maury was out of earshot, I muttered every swear word I knew eight or ten times. Then I went inside, pulled out my trunk, dug out my knapsack, and stuffed it with shirts and underwear and socks and toilet junk.

"Where you going?" Julius asked me.

"Buzz off." I wasn't in the mood to talk to anybody.

"They're sticking him in with the little kids, I bet," said Frank Schwartz. "That's what they did to me last year."

"How cute," Howard Andeker simpered. "Hope you're good at telling fairy tales."

"You can tell 'em about real fairies," Nick said. "You're an expert."

"Yeah," I said. "I'll tell 'em about you."

"Take that back," Nick commanded.

"The hell I will," I said, slinging my knapsack on my shoulder. "Boy, it'll be great to get away from all you cretins." I stormed out the door. The hell with them. The hell with everybody. Hostile? That didn't begin to cover it.

15

I got to the green-stripe cabin as the little brats were getting ready for their slimnastics session. "Hey, who are you?" asked a little blond kid who seemed scared of me. It must've been my maniacal look.

"Your new counselor," I said.

"Where's the old one?" he asked suspiciously.

"Dead."

"Like hell," said a butterball who was a couple of years away from being Nick Barris's double.

"It's true," I said. "He got permanent brain damage from being around you guys."

"Now I know who he is," said a redheaded squirt in a singsongy voice. "He's the one who screwed up and didn't get to go on the campout."

"What a loser," croaked a froggy voice from the corner.

"Okay, guys! Slimnastics time!" the counselor yelled cheerfully as he came through the door. He looked at me. "What's your name again?"

"Sam Zimmer."

"Right. I'm Mark. Guys, Sam's going to be staying with us for a couple of days, and I hope you'll make him feel welcome. Now, let's get out there for slimnastics. Sam, you can change and meet us on the field."

"I already had slimnastics today."

"He's lying," said the red-haired kid.

"Did you really have slimnastics?" their counselor asked me. I nodded. "Okay, we'll see you later on, then. Your bunk's over there. Up top. Take it easy."

"See you, loser," croaked the frog-voiced kid. He even looked like a frog. A fat one. And leaped out the door like one before I had a chance to punch him.

I tossed my knapsack onto my bunk and lay down on the one below it. This was the worst yet. There is nothing like spending time with a bunch of brats at least two grades behind you.

The really bad part was knowing they could get away with just about any trick they felt like pulling on me, because I wouldn't be around long enough to get even. I'd have to be on my guard against junk in my bed, water in my shoes, and whatever else bright little fifth- and sixth-graders could think up to bedevil their elders.

And right now my cabinmates were probably hoisting their packs onto their shoulders and hiking into the wilderness, while I got to stare up at the springs of my temporary bunk. Hell! It was too much. The straw that broke the camel's back. The end of my patience. I couldn't take it any more.

I knew what I had to do. I'd find Belinda and tell

her, yes, let's run away. Let's get out of this prison once and for all. If they find us and send us home, so much the better.

I looked at my watch. It was just past three. She might be at slimnastics, and she might be at swim class, but if she were, I wouldn't be able to talk to her anyhow. So I walked over to the crafts shed.

I was in luck. Belinda was working on some tie-dye cloth thing, dipping it into a vat of green stuff. When she took it out, it looked truly hideous. She was so busy with it, she didn't even notice me until Christina looked up from helping her and said "Hi" to me.

Belinda didn't say anything. She gave me a little salute with her free hand and went back to her project.

"What are you working on?" Christina asked me.

"Nothing."

"How'd you like to try your hand at some clay?"

"Sure. Why not?"

Christina stuck her hands into the clay pot and plopped a big drippy gray hunk in front of me. I was still halfway across the room from Belinda, so I couldn't exactly strike up a conversation with her.

But the clay turned out to be a pretty good idea. I took my frustrations out on it. First I just punched it around for a while. Then I made a hot dog, a snake, a rope, and a doughnut. Finally I reworked it all into a brilliant representational piece I called "A Lump." It ended up back in the clay pot. That's how it is with art.

I caught up with Belinda as she was leaving. "Let's talk."

"I can't," she said. "There's an all-cabin powwow now. Heap big important."

"Since when did you start worrying about that stuff?"

"Since a certain someone lectured me about my hostility."

"Hell!" I shouted. "I thought I could count on you. I want to break out."

"Eat a lot of chocolate and don't wash your face."

"Will you get serious? I want to leave. Now."

"Why the sudden change?"

"How would you like to have to room with a bunch of kindergartners for three days?"

"Yuck! You mean they actually did that to you?"

"Nowhere else to put me while the guys my age are on campout."

Belinda's eyes lit up. "Let's go into the woods a second." She was her old self again, thinking and scheming. Langer hadn't brainwashed her at all. It was more like a mild rinse.

"I've got it!" she cried, once we were in the woods. "Tomorrow night's the movie, right? Perfect time to sneak out while nobody's looking."

"How do you come up with these ideas?"

"I'm brilliant."

"It sounds brilliant, all right. All we need are some details."

"Look, Marcie's up for cabin council vice president, and she'll kill me if I don't get back there to vote for her. Meet me under the oak at three tomorrow and we'll get all the details straightened out."

"How am I going to survive a night with those brats?"

"They're just little kids. What can they do to you?"

I shrugged and made a face. "Wish I knew."

We shook hands. "Till tomorrow, comrade," she said with a little salute. Then we went our separate ways.

Back at the nursery school, everybody wanted to know how old I was.

"None of your business," I said.

"Fifteen?" somebody asked.

"Skip it," I said, inspecting my bed for sabotage.

"I'm eleven," one shrimp said. I was supposed to be impressed.

"Why don't you do whatever it is that eleven-year-olds do and quit bothering me?" I said.

"Go to hell," he replied. This younger generation is really something, I thought. I'd've never said anything like that to an older kid when I was eleven. Well, maybe if I'd been really mad . . .

"One . . . two . . . THREE!" the frog croaked. All of a sudden I was bombarded with pine cones. I fired some back, but I had to dodge seven sets of prickles at once, and I was clearly getting the worst of it. The counselor finally came in and got them to stop. They were almost out of ammunition anyhow.

"All right, you guys, clean up this mess, or stay down here and skip dinner. That's no way to treat a guest," the counselor said.

"Guest, nothing," somebody answered. "We didn't invite him. He's just a creep who got stuck here."

"Well, he has to put up with the situation, and so do you. Now, get this place in shape." The counselor went out the door.

I fired some of the pine cones from my bed at Froggy, the obvious ringleader. He started whipping them back at me.

"I don't know about you," one of the other kids said, "but I want my dinner." So did Froggy and I. We stopped the war.

But at dinner the frog deliberately spilled a glass of bug juice in my lap. He and his cabinmates thought it was the funniest thing they'd ever seen. I yanked him off the bench and started slamming him against the wall.

This is not the kind of thing I normally do. Usually I'm just an easygoing kid who lets things pass. But I guess I hadn't taken all my frustrations out on that clay after all, and the thought of this little moron humiliating me in front of everybody made me even angrier, and since he was little and I knew he wouldn't be able to fight back very hard, I just roared into action. "Cut it out!" he kept yelling, and he tried to bite me, but I kept shoving him back and forth against the wall till I felt somebody a lot bigger pull me away.

His counselor, naturally. "All right, you two. Shake hands."

Neither of us made a move.

"Shake hands. Or no canteen."

Froggy held his hand out to me, and I crunched it as hard as I could. He did the same to me, but it didn't hurt at all, since his hand was a lot smaller than mine. As we sat down again, he muttered, "You son of a bitch," just loud enough so I could hear and his counselor couldn't.

I grabbed the pitcher of bug juice and dumped it on his head. He jumped and squirmed and acted miserable. His cabinmates cracked up.

His counselor was furious. "Get out of here, Zimmer. Get down to the cabin and stay there."

"Fine," I said. So I'd miss dessert tonight. Big deal. At least I wouldn't have to sit around the campfire with these . . . these *babies*.

I went down to the cabin and changed out of my wet pants, wondering what I could do to get even with the little jerks. Then I got the bright idea of mixing up all their clothes, trading it between their drawers and messing it up while I was at it. This kept me busy for a while. Then I lay down and read a journalism book.

It was the first peace and quiet I'd had in days. I actually finished three chapters before the twerps descended on me. They were all hot and sweaty from volleyball, and Froggy was also purple from bug juice. When they noticed their drawers, they had fits. They yelled and screamed and were getting set to come at me, but their counselor stepped in and declared a truce. He said I was entitled to get even for their pine-cone attack.

It took them nearly an hour to get everything straightened out. When they finished, we all went down to the toilets to get ready for bed. At Froggy's count of three, everybody took his toothbrush out of his mouth and used it as a catapult to fling toothpaste at me.

Toothpaste really stings your eyes. I knew one thing for sure: good plan or bad, Belinda and I would be leaving this place tomorrow.

16

That old story about fat people being jolly isn't entirely a myth. Some of us have figured out that a smile tends to improve our chances of being treated like human beings. However, when I woke up that morning my stomach felt awful, my face felt like one big scab, and when I looked at myself in somebody's mirror, I didn't feel much like going "Ho, ho, ho."

"Shoot!" I said (or something pretty close to it). "Poison ivy!"

"Won't hurt *your* popularity any," said a sleepy-sounding frog.

I never did figure out exactly how they'd done it. Probably they found a piece of plastic to handle the plant with, and then brushed it over my face while I was sleeping. I remembered dreaming something about walking through a forest. That was probably when it happened. If I'd known how rotten twelve-year-olds could be, I'd've stayed awake all night.

But now it was still half an hour till reveille, and my face looked like it might fall off if it didn't get some kind of medical attention fast. I pulled on my pants, went down to the counselors' cabin, and beat on the door.

"Yeah? Who is it?" a sleepy voice moaned.

"Sam Zimmer," I said.

"Who?"

"Sam Zimmer. From the green-stripe cabin."

Muffled voices inside. "Get up, Mark," somebody said. "This one's *your* problem."

More muffled voices. Feet padding across the floor. The door unlatching. "All right," Mark yawned angrily. "What's ... My god! How'd that happen?"

"Your little darlings did it while I was asleep. I've got to get some help."

Mark took a closer look at me. "I'd better get you up to the infirmary. Let me put some clothes on."

I sat on the porch and tried to keep from scratching my itchy face. Then Mark and I went up to the infirmary. As he'd suspected, it was locked. We had to go around to good old nursie's cabin and wake her up. Fortunately it wasn't a severed artery or something. By the time I got help, I'd be dead.

The so-called nurse finally came out in her uniform and led me to the infirmary. She inspected my face. "You certainly manage to get into your share of trouble," she said.

"Not my fault I was attacked by a poison-ivy plant."

"Ha, ha," she said. She went to the medicine

cabinet, took down a bottle of pink lotion, read the label, and said, "Hmmm."

"Hmmm?"

"This is what we usually use. But it says you're not supposed to apply it near eyes or lips."

"Maybe I should see a doctor."

The nurse ignored that suggestion. Instead, she flipped through the pages of something called *The Household Medical Encyclopedia and Emergency Guide.* It was so modern and up to date it had a cover depicting a father, mother, boy, girl, and dog all standing around flashing healthy smiles at their brand new 1952 Chevy.

The nurse couldn't find what she was looking for. "I'll be back," she said, and went out the door.

I picked up the book and had a look for myself. Under "Poison Ivy," the index said to see "Contact Dermatitis," and under "Contact Dermatitis," there was a listing for "Plants." It was nice to know you could count on this book's speedy help in an emergency.

Anyhow, under "Contact Dermatitis, Plant-Induced," there was a helpful picture of a poison-ivy plant and the advice that the best thing to do was avoid it entirely. There was also a picture of a man spraying insecticide on a cluster of the plants. And at last, under "treatment," the advice I'd been waiting for: "Normally, the rash will heal itself in two to three weeks. Careful washing with yellow laundry soap will prevent the spread of the rash. Applications of calamine lotion may relieve itching. Severe cases should receive prompt medical attention."

I sat around itching and wondering how severe my case was until Miss Prompt Medical Attention herself came back with a doctor. Dr. Ira Langer. "How you doing?" he asked.

"Guess," I said.

"How did it happen?"

I shrugged. "Some people don't like outsiders."

"Well, when I get to the bottom of this, you can be sure whoever's responsible will be punished severely."

"Right now, I'd just like to be sure I get to see a doctor," I said. The nurse stuck a thermometer in my mouth.

"You're not the first person who's ever had a little poison ivy," Langer said with a reassuring grin.

"I'd still like to see a doctor," I said.

"Keep that under your tongue!" Nurse commanded. I shut my mouth.

Langer paced back and forth. He took a cigarette out of his pocket and was all set to light it when he noticed me pointing to the NO SMOKING sign on the wall. He hesitated for a second, then lit up anyway. Just to show who was boss.

The nurse frowned at my temperature and showed it to Langer. "How bad is it?" I asked.

"You have a mild fever," Langer said.

"How mild?"

"Don't worry. I'm going to call the doctor right now." He walked out the door.

"How high is it?" I asked the nurse.

"Not too high."

"Come on. How high?"

"A hundred and two."

"That's not what I'd call 'mild.'"

"Lie down and rest. The doctor will be here soon." She gave me a look that meant she devoutly wished she had a job where she wouldn't have to put up with kids. Then she left. All I had to read was the label on the side of the rollaway nightstand. I fell asleep.

A masculine "Hmmm" woke me up again. I opened my eyes and saw a gaunt stringbean of a man with a crinkly face staring at me. "This is Dr. Wallingford," Langer said helpfully.

"Got yourself quite a case," the doctor said. "How do you feel?"

"Not so hot."

"You're hot, all right, with that fever of yours. I'm going to give you something for that, and an ointment for that rash. Now, I want you to take it easy for a few days. Stay out of the sun, use the medications, don't overexert yourself. You should be fine."

Don't ask me why at this moment of all moments the thought came to me. It just did. "How about eating?"

"Nothing special. Your normal routine."

"Around here that's like two calories a day."

"Oh." He turned to Dr. Langer. "I don't think we should be at all concerned about his losing weight until the rash subsides. He should eat normally." The doctor turned back to me. "Which is not to say you should turn into a glutton. Everything in moderation for the next week or so. And stay out of that sun."

He wrote out two prescriptions and handed them to Langer. "Have these filled in town. Be sure to call me if there are any complications."

Dr. Wallingford shook my hand, told me to take it easy, and left the room. Langer followed him. The nurse stayed behind and glared at me.

"Well!" I said, suddenly feeling a whole lot better. "What's for breakfast?"

17

"You big fat hog," Belinda growled.

"Look who's talking!" I said.

"You'll be fatter than ever if you don't get off your butt soon." She leaned over the bed and tried to yank my milkshake from my hand. I drew it away from her. Actually, it wasn't a real milkshake, a fresh one with ice cream and milk and syrup. It was one of those canned ones with thickeners and preservatives and carrageenan and guar gum and chemicals about as palatable as they are pronounceable. Compared to what you got in the mess hall, it was terrific.

"Come on! Just one sip," Belinda pleaded.

"Off-limits except for us invalids."

"You bastard! First you fink out on me after I work up this incredible plan, and now you won't even give me a sip of your shake."

"Hey, not so loud! For all I know, they may be bugging this room."

"Just one little sip," she begged. You've never seen a more pitiful look on anybody's face.

I handed her the cup. She took a sip and made the kind of face you only see in TV commercials when somebody bites into some incredible new improved

134

awful product. Only with her it wasn't an act. It was pure joy. She looked as though she'd be delighted to die with that flexible straw in her mouth. When I'd taken my first sip of that chemical concoction, I'd felt exactly the same way.

"Give it back." I hated to break up her love affair with the shake, but it'd taken me a lot of effort to get it, and I certainly wasn't about to let her drink it all.

"One more swallow."

"No!"

Belinda closed her eyes in rapture and took one anyway. Then she handed me the cup as though she could hardly bear to part with it. She considerately left me at least two good sips.

I scowled. "I wonder if poison ivy can be transmitted through drinking straws."

"Oh, stop it. Compared to the rest of us, you're on the gravy train."

Of course, she was right. And all because I'd asked that doctor the right question. Langer had grudgingly told the nurse to get me whatever I wanted from the counselors' mess as long as it didn't go over twenty-five hundred calories a day. So I was eating counselor food, the very same stuff Langer and his minions ate all the time after pretending to enjoy their aluminized, portion-controlled dog dinners. It was almost wonderful.

I was allowed visitors only during active rest and right after dinner, so that the nurse could keep an eye on me while I ate and prevent me from corrupting the morals and stomachs of the visitors by offering them something caloric. However, Belinda so desperately wanted to be corrupted that she'd sneaked into the infirmary while the nurse was out to lunch.

"So how long are you in for?" Belinda asked, licking the last drop of my milkshake from her upper lip.

"At least a week."

"God! When'll we do our disappearing act?"

"We won't have to. After this, I think I can convince my parents to take me home."

"I thought you said they were going to Europe."

"They'll figure something out. Anyhow, we'd never have gotten very far."

"Zimmer, I planned the escape down to the last detail."

"Shhh. I told you, we might be bugged."

She lowered her voice. "Among other things, we use a boat so they can't follow our trail."

"And then what, without food or money? Eat the boat?"

"There's another camp just down a ways on the other side of the lake. What we do is get the kids there to give us some stuff from their canteen."

"Sure. They're gonna help some poor starving fat kids from Camp Thin-na-Yet."

"My second cousin will. She's over there, and she's in charge of the canteen this week, and she knows if she doesn't help, I'll brain her. I already wrote her and everything. It was all set."

"Belinda, forget it. I'm just going to lie here till visitors' day and let my parents take me home."

"Who says?"

"I says."

"Bet they won't."

"They will."

She shook her head disgustedly. "Look, gutless, I want to get out of here. If you won't help me, I'll find someone who will."

"Go ahead. The only thing you've helped me do is make my milkshake disappear."

"See you around." She got up to leave.

"Belinda?" I called.

She turned toward me. "Yeah?"

"Listen, I really did want to break out of here with you. I'm sorry this screwed everything up."

"*You're* sorry!"

I nodded. "Come visit me again? Please? It's really lonely in here."

"I guess you've forgotten what it's like out there." She huffed out the door.

The next few days were about as exciting as watching trees grow. Langer never did find out which of the green-stripers were responsible for my rash, so he made them all come by and apologize. He needn't've bothered. All they did was stand at my bedside and say "We're sorry," and "We're really sorry," and "We sure are sorry," in the snottiest tones you could imagine. The minute they got out the door, they all exploded in a fit of giggles. I had an almost uncontrollable urge to wring their necks, but

I wasn't supposed to get out of bed except to go to the bathroom.

My cabin didn't hear anything about me till they got back from their campout. Then they all came for a visit. Considering our wisecracks when Frank had been sick, I didn't really expect a whole lot of sympathy, and they did make a lot of jokes about posion ivy and what happens when you miss your weight-loss goal and stuff like that. On the other hand, they did ask if there was anything they could do. I couldn't think of much. Maury lent me his radio on a semi-permanent basis, but that was about it.

Julius hung around for a while. From his description, the campout wasn't exactly as much fun as everybody had expected. The canoe trip was a lot of work, and after that and a five-mile hike through the forest, everybody was tired and cranky and hungry. But the hamburgers were about as thick as birch bark, and the marshmallows didn't even taste as good as pillow stuffing. And the bugs were fierce. Worst of all, there was a Dairy Queen right down the road from the "wilderness" where they were camping, and since nobody had any money, all they could do was lie awake all night and watch a huge plastic ice-cream cone twirl around at the top of a tall pole and torment them.

Julius also helped me out with a very important mission. I had written my parents the letter I was sure would mean my freedom. It was seven pages long, and told them calmly and rationally all the reasons why I wanted to go home. I wrote it twice, first as a rough draft, and then in a final version I was careful to do in a big, legible script. Everybody usually calls my handwriting "chicken scratch," so I figured this sudden neatness would help prove to my parents that something was desperately wrong with me.

The hard part was getting the thing mailed. Since it wasn't the kind of letter you wanted to put on a postcard for everybody to look at, and it wouldn't've fit anyhow, I wrote it on notebook paper and borrowed an envelope from the nurse's desk when she wasn't looking. But the only place you could get stamps was the canteen, and I wasn't allowed out of bed. I asked Julius to buy some stamps and mail the letter for me. He said he'd be glad to.

"Whatever you do, don't give it to Maury," I said. "He might pass it on to Langer."

"If he tries, I'll jump on his toes."

Julius was okay. I offered him a cupcake I'd stashed away for later. He actually refused it. Winning that weight-loss crown apparently had worked some magical effect on him. Which was fine with me. I wanted that cupcake myself.

As he disappeared with the letter, I started worrying about what my parents might say to it. Like "No." But after this poison-ivy business, I couldn't see how they could possibly refuse to take me home. When I told Belinda about it, she said I was dreaming.

Whenever Belinda dropped by, I always seemed

139

to spend the first five minutes defending my food from her attacks and the last five minutes insisting I really wasn't going to run away with her. But I was always glad to see her. Her snideness and sarcasm cheered me up somehow.

Finally my rash began to get better. The doctor's magic cream really kept the itching down. The only trouble was that he didn't prescribe a cream for boredom. "Hell! I want to get out of here!" I yelled at the nurse on my fifth day of bedriddenness after losing my fifteenth straight hand of solitaire.

"We're supposed to keep you under observation."

"You can observe all you want. I just want to get up and around again."

"You'll have to take that up with Dr. Langer."

"Okay, I will," I said, swinging my legs over the side of the bed.

"You stay put," she said with one of her patented frowns, and went out the door.

I got out of bed and found my clothes. Just getting dressed felt terrific. I strolled outside. Langer was headed my way.

"Where do you think you're going?" he demanded.

"For a walk," I said.

"You're supposed to keep out of the sun."

"I'll stay in the shade."

He put a paw on my shoulder. "Sam, why do you have to be so hostile? First you want a doctor. We get you a doctor. He tells you to stay inside. So you run around out here. Don't you think anybody beside yourself has any sense?"

"I'm staying out of the sun. I know my face is messed up bad enough without my disobeying doctor's orders. But what he said was, 'Take it easy.' I'm not planning to do any slimnastics, if that's what you're worried about."

"You're feeling better, then?"

"Yeah. A lot."

"All right," Langer said. "You made your point. Just keep out of that sun."

"Right."

"But as long as you're well enough to get up, you're well enough to eat in the mess hall with the rest of us."

"I'm not *that* well. You heard what the doctor said about my diet."

"I spoke with him yesterday. He said that he saw nothing wrong in your going back on a reducing diet once you felt strong enough to get up and walk around. I'm glad you're well. You can go back to your cabin. Just stay out of the sun and don't get your rash on anyone else's clothes or sheets. And now, if you'll excuse me, I'm due at the tennis court." He walked away.

Well, all good things must come to an end. But so, I told myself, must the bad ones. I'd be going home on visitors' day for sure. Just eight more rotten aluminum feasts, and I'd be gone from this place for good.

18

I got back to the cabin so suddenly the only thing anybody'd had a chance to do was short-sheet my bed. Aside from a lot of jokes about staying out of people's way because they didn't want to get poison ivy or cooties, nothing much had changed.

Next afternoon, I got a letter from home. I took it to the john with me and ripped it open. It was typed, and it was long. It had to be the good news I was waiting for.

Dear Sam:

Your long letter came in the morning mail. I must say it was easier to read than your usual scrawl. Are they teaching penmanship up there, or did you dictate it to somebody?

Dr. Langer phoned to notify us about your poison ivy, so we were aware of the problem even before you wrote. Dr. Langer said you were getting the best of medical care and observation and that you were expected to make a quick recovery. He said he'd let us know if there were any problems, but we haven't heard from him since, so I assume you're healing well and will soon be running around again if you're not already.

As to your other complaints, I must say they

142

seem rather petty, though I can see how from your point of view they might look different. Still, fine cuisine is something you just don't expect at any camp, and I can't imagine your "TV dinners" are any worse than most. I often have to eat that stuff on airplanes when I fly on business, and though I admit it's not Escoffier or Julia Child, it's never made me jump out of the plane in protest.

A lot of your grievances seem no worse than things you described about the camp you went to two years ago, which, as I recall, you seem to have survived. If memory serves, that camp didn't even offer you your choice of activities. So while I sympathize with your feelings about the shortage of archery equipment, I do have to point out that however little the camp may have, it's more than we've got here at home.

When we spoke with him the other night, Dr. Langer said you were extremely hostile toward camp in general and him in particular. He felt that this hostility was the main thing that kept you from meeting your weight goal and put you in the position of having to room with those kids (rotten, I grant you) who dosed you up with the poison ivy. In other words, he thinks a number of your troubles are of your own making, and I'm afraid I have to agree.

Sometimes it's a good idea to walk away from situations you don't like. But sometimes it's better to stick it out and see how you can make the best of it. Unfortunately, there are quite a few situations you can't walk away from. For example, a number of the people I work with happen to be extremely unpleasant, but since I'm not in a

143

position to fire them, I have to do my best to get along with them five days a week, forty-nine weeks a year. You've run into similar problems in school, so you know what I'm talking about. I'm not going to go into a long sermon about it.

Mom and I are very pleased that you've lost ten pounds or thereabouts already, and we really think you should see this through. Our forthcoming trip has nothing to do with that decision, by the way. We've discussed the whole matter pretty thoroughly, and we'll be glad to talk about it with you when we see you on visitors' day. Which we're looking forward to.

Love,
Dad

P.S. Don't think you're alone. Even your old parents are dieting these days. It isn't easy, as I guess I don't have to tell you, but we've lost a couple pounds each so far, and we're already feeling better.

Dad

It wasn't good news at all. It was just a nice rational answer to my nice rational letter. But I did something that wasn't particularly rational: I cried.

I cried a lot. I couldn't help it. Tears streamed down my face and dripped onto my bare legs. Everything was wrong.

I don't know how long I kept at it. Somebody's footsteps were coming toward the door, so I wiped my tears on my shirt and buried my face in my hands. The tears stopped, but I kept on sobbing. The person who came in used the urinal and left. I tried to pull myself together, but just when I thought I'd made it, another wave of sobs swept me up.

Finally I drained myself dry. I went outside and stuck my head under the faucet. The cold water felt good.

I dried off on my T-shirt and headed for the woods. It was active rest period and somebody'd probably come looking for me, but I didn't care. If I went back to the cabin, I'd have to handle a million questions about whether I'd been crying and why I'd been crying and what kind of fairy I was to go around crying anyhow, and right now I couldn't cope with that. I had to sort things out a little.

I found a fallen tree to sit on. I reread the letter. The trouble was that it all seemed so sensible. My problems *were* trivial. My poison ivy *was* healing. The food *hadn't* killed me. I *did* get to shoot a bow and arrow once in a while. I *was* getting thinner. What was so terrible?

I was miserable, that's what. My father just sort of ignored all the little points, the things like isolation and tyrannical rules and lack of privacy that made Camp Thin-na-Yet seem like Camp Concentration to me. Sometimes you can't condense the world into a letter.

It's like when you meet somebody who's good-looking and well-dressed and smart and pleasant and everything and yet somehow you know that this particular person is just a rotten human being.

There's nothing to put your finger on except maybe an insincere tone of voice or a slightly phony smile, but you just know this person isn't somebody you could be friends with. Sometimes you just have to trust your feelings.

And despite Dad's letter, my feeling about Camp Thin-na-Yet was that I couldn't possibly take another three weeks of it. I started thinking about Belinda's plan to run away, and I realized it'd be impossible. But then I decided to do something that was even harder.

"What now?" Langer asked as I came through the door to his office.

"I want to phone my father," I said.

"I thought we had that all settled. You had your chance, and you chose not to."

"I want to phone my father."

"Is there some problem?"

This time the sorcerer wouldn't beat me. I was a mule. "I want to phone my father."

"I'd really like to know what's troubling you."

"I want to phone my father."

"I thought you said you didn't want to phone him at work."

"I want to phone my father."

"I'd appreciate it if you stopped acting like a broken record."

"I want to phone my father."

"Zimmer, I've had enough of you! Here! Phone him!" Langer spat, thrusting the phone at me. My record may have been broken, but it communicated all right.

"Thank you," I said. I dialed "1" and the area code and the number. "I'd like some privacy."

"What are you afraid I'll hear?"

"I'd like some privacy." Same record; I just moved the needle up a groove.

"Let me know when you're through." Langer went out the door. It squooshed shut behind him.

"VCP Industries," said a woman at the other end of the line.

"Irving Zimmer, please," I said. I got a buzzy sound for a while.

"Zimmer here." Dad always answered the phone that way at work.

"Hi, Dad. How are you?" I spoke in a low voice, cupping my hand over the mouthpiece. It was a cool day, and the windows were wide open. I didn't want Langer listening in.

"Sam! Are you okay?" Dad asked.

"No."

"What's the trouble?"

"The trouble is, I hate it up here."

"Speak up a little. I can't hear you."

"I said, I hate it here."

"Did you get my letter?"

"Yeah."

"Didn't I get my point across?"

"Yeah, you did, but I don't think you got mine. This camp is horrible."

147

"Oh, it can't be all *that* bad."

"It's worse. I've been here nearly three weeks now, I hated it from the minute I got here, and I hate it worse each day. It's like being in prison."

"I can't believe that."

"It's not something you can describe in a letter. You'd have to be here and live through it."

"Sam, I just can't imagine things are as bad as you make them out to be."

"I'm not the only one who feels this way. Kids have even asked me to run away with them."

"That's not a very smart idea."

"I know. But what other choice is there if your parents won't listen to you?"

Dad let out a long sigh. "Don't you think you should give it a little better try? Your attitude can't be so hot if all you can think about is leaving."

"It's nothing to do with my attitude. You and Mom walk out of movies when they're rotten, because you don't want to waste any more time being bored or insulted. It's the same thing here. Only it's worse than any movie you ever saw. And it's not just an hour and a half. It's a whole summer."

"I'd really like you to work this out."

"I'd like to, too. But I can't lie and say everything's great when it isn't. I didn't even want to come here in the first place."

Dad sighed again. There was a long silence. Finally he came back on the line. "Is Dr. Langer around?"

"Yeah, right outside."

"Could you put him on?"

"Okay, but I want to talk with you again when you're through."

"Sure."

"Hang on a minute."

I went to the window. Langer was hanging around beneath it. It was obviously the best place for him to try and listen in on me. "My dad wants to talk to you," I said.

Langer came in. "Mind waiting outside?"

I shrugged. There was nothing to keep me from eavesdropping at the window myself. So that's what I did.

"Well, Mr. Zimmer. How are you? . . . Fine. What seems to be the trouble? . . . I see. Of course, he wouldn't tell me. For some reason, he doesn't trust me."

Very perceptive, I thought.

"I see. . . . How do you feel about it? . . . I see. . . . Well, we don't normally . . . Still, that's not our usual policy. . . . True, that was something of a special circumstance. . . . But it does say on the application, 'nonrefundable.' "

Nonrefundable? I jumped in the air and let out a silent whoop. I was going home!

"Why don't we discuss it when you're here in person? . . . Yes, certainly."

Langer came back outside with a frown on his face. It was the exact opposite of how I looked.

149

"Your father wants to talk with you again," he said.

I went inside and picked up the phone. "Hi," I said cheerfully.

"Sam, in some ways this goes against my better judgment, but I've spoken with Dr. Langer and, okay, you can come home. You're sure, now?"

"Boy, am I."

"You can hang on till Sunday, can't you?"

"By the skin of my teeth. Why don't you ask Langer to give me some decent food in the meantime?"

"Aw, come on, Sam. The guy's already furious with me. Eat what they give you, and Sunday we'll go out for a big noon dinner."

"I thought you were on a diet."

"I guess your homecoming's a good enough excuse to break it."

"I hope this doesn't mess up your trip."

"It won't make things any easier, that's for sure. We'll figure something out."

"Listen, Dad, thanks. You can't imagine how horrible it is up here."

"You're right. I can't. But if you feel that strongly about it, it's your decision. You may as well have at least half a summer to look forward to. Now, how about letting me do a little work around here? See you Sunday?"

"Right. Thanks again."

"Hey! How's that poison ivy?"

"Itchy. Getting better."

"Good. Okay. See you Sunday."

We hung up. I remembered I probably should've told him to say hello to Mom for me, but it was too late to do anything about it now.

Langer came in. "So we're going to lose you, Sam?"

"Yup."

"It's a shame that a bright kid like you is such a quitter. It's the kind of attitude that won't be much help to you in life situations."

"Yeah, well." Yesterday I'd've argued with him, told him you're not a quitter when you get out of a bad situation you can't do anything to change, but right now all I wanted to do was get out of there.

"We've helped quite a few people with their problems over the past few years. We've been responsible for a total weight loss of nearly two tons."

"Uh-huh." I restrained myself from saying he could add in my seven pounds if it'd make him feel better.

"Please do me one favor," Langer said.

"What's that?"

"Try to stay out of trouble between now and visitors' day."

"Sure. Anything else?"

"I'll speak with your counselor about packing your things and getting back your laundry. You can go."

I went. The sky seemed bluer, the air smelled fresher, the birds sang louder. My head felt as though somebody'd lifted an enormous concrete block from it. There's more than one way to feel lighter.

19

Somehow you always feel happiest right after you've finished feeling rotten. Say you expect to do well on a test and then you do—you feel okay, but it's not anything special. But if you're sweating and worrying about flunking that test because you haven't studied for it, and then it turns out you know every answer anyway, you get this incredible feeling of relief and I guess what you'd call euphoria. Which is how I felt, only multiplied about a hundred thousand times, as I headed back to the cabin. Even my rash seemed better.

"Maury wants to see you," Bernie Androsky said as I stepped through the door.

"Where were you, anyhow?" Julius wanted to know.

I grinned. "In Langer's office."

"More trouble?" Julius asked.

"Not exactly."

"So what happened?"

"What happened is I'm going home on visitors' day," I announced. Everybody was suddenly struck dumb.

"No kidding?" Julius finally asked.

"Would I lie to you?"

"Aw. Wittle Sammy couldn't take it," Nick baby-talked.

"Wittle Sammy is going to be eating like a hog day after tomorrow, while Big Nicky starves on baby food," I said.

"How'd you manage it?" Julius wanted to know.

"I called my dad and told him what a load of crap this place is."

"Langer let you?" Frank Schwartz couldn't believe it.

"I had to persuade him."

"Zimmer, you've got a lot of guts," Andeker said.

"And a nice guy for a father," said Nick Barris.

Maury bounded up the stairs. "All right, guys! Slimnastics in five minutes!" He noticed me. "Zimmer, where were you?"

"Up talking to Langer."

"You're supposed to let me know where you are, not go traipsing off like that. Besides, you can't go bothering Dr. Langer for every little thing. That's what the counselors are here for."

"If you're going to punish him, better do it quick," Andeker said. "He's leaving day after tomorrow."

"What?" Maury cried.

"I just talked with my father. I'm going home on visitors' day. Langer said you'd help me get straightened out with my laundry and packing."

Maury looked stunned. "How come you never said

153

anything to me about this before? Jeez, this makes me look stupid."

"You said it, I didn't," I said. I heard some laughs behind me.

"All right, clowns. Slimnastics. Four minutes. Move it." Maury left.

I was still under orders to stay out of the sun, so slimnastics and swimming and even archery were out of the picture for me. I decided to take a stroll through the woods.

It was funny. Everything had changed so suddenly, I hadn't had time to adjust. Here I was, almost used to eating three and only three times a day, brushing my teeth with half a dozen other people, and being totally cut off from the outside world, and now I was going to get back to my usual at-home routine. It wasn't unpleasant, but it sure felt strange.

"Haven't seen you in a while," Christina said when I entered the crafts shed.

"I was in the infirmary." I noticed Belinda standing over the tie-dye vat with her back toward me.

"How you feeling?" Christina asked.

"Okay."

"Want to try making a pot?"

"Sure."

Christina set me up at the potter's wheel and showed me what to do. It was kind of fun, though I obviously will never have the coordination to be a great potter. I ruined my pots twice glancing over at Belinda, who looked very serious as she dipped her

154

ugly green fabric into a pot of purple dye, trying to break the record for most awful-looking design. Just before cleanup time, I actually got the hang of the wheel, and I came up with a very ordinary but kind of cute little vase. "I'll put it in the kiln," Christina said. "You can glaze it tomorrow."

"Thanks," I said, looking around for Belinda. She had disappeared.

I went out the door to look for her. I didn't have far to search. She was waiting for me.

"Let's go into the woods," she said. We headed up the path to our spot near the oak tree.

"Your face looks a lot better," she told me.

"Thanks. I've got some great news."

Her face broke into a big smile. "Well, about time! When are you ready to sneak out?"

"I'm not. My parents are taking me home on visitors' day."

"Dream on."

"Seriously. I talked to my dad this morning."

"By mental telepathy?"

"By Langer's telephone. It's all settled. Except for whether Langer'll give us a refund."

Belinda looked stunned. "God!" She shook her head.

"Why don't you try it?"

"You don't know *my* parents."

"What harm could it do?"

"They wouldn't even listen. All that'd happen is Langer would bill them for the call, and then they'd take it out on me somehow."

"What's the alternative?"

Belinda looked as though somebody had hit her hard. "You know what it is. I'm stuck here, that's what."

"You could still break out."

"Did I ever say I could do it alone?" Belinda looked as though she might start crying.

"Look on the bright side. At least you're losing weight."

"Yeah. I guess."

"Listen, we ought to write to each other or something."

"As long as you don't tell me anything about what you're eating. God, you're lucky."

"I know."

Suddenly she pulled me toward her and kissed me on the lips. Not that I was an expert, but this was really an unusual kind of kiss, very passionate and very desperate, as if she were going to break into tears the next second. I put my arm around her and started to pull her toward me, but she broke free and ran away. I didn't even have a chance to give her my address. I hoped she wouldn't get my poison ivy from that kiss.

The rest of that day and the next went by in a flash. I kept busy getting everything rounded up and stuffed back into my footlocker, which was pretty easy because the camp somehow had misplaced my last load of laundry, and without it, everything fit just fine.

My pot had come out okay, and I spent part of the afternoon glazing it. I decided I'd pick it up next morning and give it to Belinda as a going-away present. She seemed really down when I spotted her in mess hall, and I thought the pot might cheer her up a little.

The week's special privilege was a movie again, but since all the little kids were away on overnights, it was a PG one. A horror film. Of course, what with all the junk I'd eaten and all the exercise I'd missed while I was in the infirmary, I didn't even come close to meeting the goal, so I couldn't see the movie.

But starting tomorrow, I could see any film I wanted, so I didn't much care about missing this one. The week's real losers were Androsky and Duff, who hit the wall exactly the same way I had. They both had wanted to see this movie ever since it came out, but instead they had to stay back in the cabin with me and play cards. They were absolutely miserable all evening until everybody else got back and told us what a boring film it was.

"What'd you expect?" Frank Schwartz said. "Langer won't show films with sex or violence in them. Parents might complain."

"What made this film a PG, anyhow?" Julius wondered.

"Don't you remember?" Frank said. "Somebody said 'Holy shit.' Twice, in fact."

"Yeah, you can't say that in a G film," Nick said.

"Why not? Everybody says 'shit,' " Julius insisted. "Even little kids say 'shit.' "

"You can say 'shit,' " Andeker explained, "as long as it's not holy. Shit's natural. Holy shit's sacrilegious."

Then we got into a big discussion of what you could say in a PG film and what you couldn't show in an R film and what you could show in an X film, and we got ready for bed and talked about it some more, and the next thing, we were asleep.

The next thing after that, it was morning. Visitors' day. It sounded like they'd bought a new record of "Reveille" just for the occasion.

20

It began pretty much like any other day. But once we got to the mess hall, things began to change in a hurry. Outside, Dr. Langer, Miss Shirt, and a couple of the girls' counselors were huddled together. They were waving and pointing and carrying on in a way that made it pretty clear they were worried about something. But it didn't concern us, obviously—probably just a hassle about whether to let the fathers visit the girls' cabins while their underwear was hanging out to dry, Nick said—so we all went in to breakfast.

While we were forcing it down, Langer mounted the stage and made an announcement. "I'd like to see all the counselors outside, please, immediately. We have a small emergency."

"You're excused," Andeker said as Maury got up and left. The counselorless mess hall turned to pandemonium.

"Wonder what this is all about," Russ Duff said.

"Maybe they found rats with bubonic plague," Frank Schwartz said. "That happened in California last year."

"No chance," Andeker said. "It has to be something utterly idiotic. Nothing interesting like plague would ever happen around here."

I looked around to see where all the counselors had gone, and then I noticed Belinda wasn't at her table. Of course, she might've just been sick. But I was sure she wasn't.

Langer and the counselors came back. "What's going on?" Julius asked.

"May I have your attention?" Langer said into the mike. "May I have everyone's attention." The noise slowly died down.

"One of our campers is missing. If we don't find her soon, we'll have to call in the authorities. So if anybody knows anything about the whereabouts of Belinda Moss—that's Be-lin-da Moss—please let your counselor know immediately. If any of you saw her at any time after lights-out last night, report it to your counselor right now."

There was a moment's silence. Langer shut off the mike. Then a giant murmur rolled through the room.

"Anybody know anything about her?" Maury asked.

Nobody did. Including me. I felt uncomfortable about not speaking up, but I wasn't going to squeal on her. And when you came right down to it, I didn't know any more about Belinda's whereabouts than anybody else. Well, a little more, maybe, assuming she was still sticking to her plan about the boat. But there was no reason to assume she would stick to that plan. After all, it was nearly a week old by now, and

Belinda knew I knew it, so maybe she'd changed it.

And what if she hadn't run away at all? What if some mad kidnaper stole her away in the middle of the night when she got up to pee? Not that it was any too likely, but you do hear about these things. If I mentioned Belinda's escape plan, the camp might delay getting outside help, and the kidnaper might cart her across the border into Canada.

But I was positive Belinda had run away. It was her flair for the dramatic. What better time to disappear than visitors' day, when there was no way Langer could possibly cover it up? He'd look like an utter idiot in front of all the parents. It was a stroke of genius.

I looked toward where Belinda usually sat. Her friend Marcie was saying something to the others. All I could make out was, "I told you, I'm a heavy sleeper," and somebody else saying, "Heavy is right."

"May I have your attention again?" Langer's voice echoed across the room. "Attention, please?"

The room hushed.

"Counselors, do you have any information to report?"

The room stayed hushed.

"Campers, I repeat again. If any of you have any information about Belinda Moss, please let us know immediately." He sounded a trifle frantic.

Nobody stirred.

"All right. Thank you." Langer jumped down from the platform and hurried out the door.

After breakfast we went down to the cabin to

make it presentable, but Maury came back a few minutes later and led us up to the mess hall again. Flashers blinking, three sheriff's cars were parked on the lawn. Kids were swarming around them.

Once all the cabins finally arrived, one of the officers climbed up to the roof of his car and shouted through a bullhorn. "All right, can I have your attention?" he yelled in a tone that meant everybody'd better shut up fast. Everybody did.

"Has anyone here seen Belinda Moss since last night?"

Nobody answered.

"Does anyone know where she might be?"

My stomach made a funny noise, but my mouth said exactly as much as everybody else's.

"All right. We're going to conduct a search. We've divided the camp into areas, and each cabin will be responsible for sweeping one area. Now, we want you to keep your eyes open in the woods, because the young lady may be in there somewhere. Miss Moss is four feet eleven inches and weighs approximately one hundred and forty-two pounds."

"Approximately!" Howard Andeker snorted.

"She has gray eyes, and was last seen wearing a yellow nightgown."

"Wonder if it's see-through," Nick mused.

"Hope not," said Andeker.

"All right, now," boomed the sheriff. "Your counselors will instruct you in what to do."

We gathered around Maury. He told us we were

162

responsible for the path from our cabin to the lake. We were supposed to walk down slowly and keep our eyes peeled, half of us looking to one side and half to the other, for any sign of Belinda.

Of course, we didn't find her. When we got to the lake, we met one of the girls' cabins coming from their path. They hadn't found Belinda, either.

I looked toward the dock. Two rowboats, three canoes, and half a dozen little sailboats were bobbing up and down in the flat waves. I didn't know how many of each there were supposed to be. I wondered if anybody'd think to check. Nobody did.

I started feeling guilty again and thought about what might've happened if Belinda'd stolen a boat and fallen out. She probably wasn't much of a swimmer. But if her plan went right, she'd be across the lake and ashore by now. And if she'd goofed up somehow, she'd've already drowned. No sense opening my mouth. But there were a million ways her plan could've failed and only two or three it could've worked. I was worried.

Belinda picked the right day to vanish, though, no question about it. As the campers got back to the lawn, parents were beginning to trickle in. Naturally, the first thing they asked about was why all the sheriff's cars were there. When they found out, they'd latch on to some other parents to talk it over with and say things like "How awful!"

My parents were among the early ones. "Hey, Sam!" my dad's voice shouted, and I turned to see him and Mom coming toward me across the lawn. We shook hands. Mom was about to kiss me when I said, "Watch out. Poison ivy."

"Let me see," she said, and turned my face in both directions. "Seems to be healing," she declared.

"Why all the cops?" Dad asked.

"One of the campers disappeared," I said.

"My god!" Mom shrieked. "Anybody you know?"

"I danced with her a couple times."

"A girl, hm?" Mom said. "Do they have any idea where she is?"

"Not a clue."

"Didn't you mention something about kids planning to run away?" Dad asked.

The last thing I needed right now was for a deputy sheriff or somebody to overhear something about how I knew about somebody's getaway plans. "She might've been kidnaped or something," I said.

"That is terrible," Mom said. "Maybe you're right about this place."

"Just another wonderful aspect of Camp Thinna-Yet," I joked.

"I suppose there's no point in my asking if you still want to come home," Mom said.

"Nope."

"Where are your things?"

"They're supposed to be up by the parking lot."

Dad looked across the grass. Langer was surrounded by half a dozen men in sheriff's uniforms plus a lot of worried parents. "I have the feeling this

164

isn't the best time to discuss our refund," Dad decided.

"Maybe we should pack my stuff in the car first," I suggested.

We went over to the parking lot and looked all around. My things weren't there. Forgotten, obviously, in all the confusion. Dad went and talked with Maury, and Maury had a discussion with Miss Shirt, and she got somebody with a truck to go down the hill for my trunk and stuff.

Meanwhile, the Mosses showed up. Belinda's parents. I didn't know who they were at first, when they were walking around looking for their kid like everybody else, but then I heard Mrs. Moss say, "Oh, god *damn* it!" and saw Mr. Moss pushing his way through the crowd, saying "I'm the lost girl's father," over and over so that people would let him past.

Mr. and Mrs. Moss were both dressed in really expensive-looking summer suits, and they looked more angry than worried. One or the other of them kept shouting "Well, what are you doing about it?" or "There must be something you can do!" or "Certainly this can't go on!" It would've been pretty much what you expected from anybody, except somehow the Mosses gave you the impression they were more concerned about showing their superiority to everybody than they were about finding their kid. For the first time since I'd met Belinda, I actually felt sorry for her.

"How *do* you find somebody in woods like these?" Mom wondered.

"Beats me," Dad said. "I'm sure she'll turn up."

The bags arrived and we loaded them into the car. "Are you sure you have everything?" Mom wanted to know.

"I'd better go down to the cabin and make sure."

"You want us to come with you?"

"Don't worry," I laughed. "I won't run away."

The cabin was empty when I got there. So were my closet and drawers. My bed was stripped. I took a last look around. There was absolutely nothing of mine in the cabin. Nothing was there to remind me of Belinda, either, but I suddenly got a sad feeling about not being able to say goodbye to her. Then I remembered my pot.

I bounded down the steps and up the path to the crafts shed. My vase was ready. "I think it looks pretty nice," Christina said. I did, too.

On the way up toward the mess hall, I kept staring into the woods, hoping Belinda might be there. I stopped at the oak tree, half expecting to see her huddled up under our saplings. But she wasn't.

And she'd made her absence felt. The chaos up on the lawn was ten times as bad as it had been the first day of camp. Sheriffs and deputies kept coming and going, parents and kids exchanged worried remarks, and Langer looked as though he might die of exhaustion any second.

"Did you make that?" Mom asked when she saw my vase.

"I had a little help."

"I never knew you had any talent for that sort of thing. I have a perfect plant for it."

"I was kind of figuring on giving it to somebody," I said.

"Oh? Who?"

"I don't know. It might make a nice gift."

"Suit yourself," Mom said.

"Do we have everything in the car now?" Dad wanted to know.

"Yup," I said.

"Well, say your goodbyes, then," Mom said. "We'll meet you here."

I found Bernie and Russ and Frank at various ends of the lawn. They were standing with their parents, waiting for the latest news on the search. Each of them introduced me as "The guy I was telling you about. The one who's leaving today."

Howard Andeker gave me a bored little wave, so I didn't see any point in doing anything else but waving back.

"Hey, Sam, be sure to write," Julius told me.

"As long as you write back."

Mr. House shook my hand. "See?" he said cheerfully. "I told you you didn't belong here. You come visit us some time, and my son the king will cook you a dinner that is out of this world."

I laughed and headed toward our car. Ten screaming kids jumped out of a station wagon in front of me. They all ran after Nick Barris.

I waved goodbye to Nick, and he waved back.

Then he good-naturedly gave me the finger. His father saw it and clobbered him in the head. Then the rest of his family surrounded him.

"Belted?" Dad asked, once we were in the car.

"Yup."

"Next stop, lunch!"

We bounced up the road. I didn't look back once. Leaving Camp Thin-na-Yet felt terrific. At least until a sheriff's car squeezed past us on the dirt road and I thought I heard the radio squawk the word "drowned."

21

Plate after plate of macaroni salad and potato salad and marinated herring and pickled beets and corn relish and huge bowls of greens with gobs and globs of dressing . . . When the restaurant owners saw me go back for my fifth helping at the all-you-can-eat salad bar, they looked worried I might bankrupt them. Much to my embarrassment, my mom told them which camp I was on the way home from. They understood perfectly.

I had no trouble at all finishing my enormous cut of roast beef and my baked potato with sour cream, not to mention part of Mom's, and I scarfed down two big hunks of peach cobbler a la mode. Considering how my waistline had shrunk, it was one of my better performances.

But what about Belinda? That's what kept gnawing at me in place of the hunger pangs of camp. All the way home, I wondered about her. At night I dreamt about her, crazy dreams and funny dreams and sexy dreams. And horrifying ones: for all I knew, she might be dead.

I did what I could to find out. At home, I dashed off a letter to Julius, telling him I hoped he was doing well up there and giving him a little report about what I was up to and asking him, sort of off-handedly so he wouldn't think it was serious between Belinda and me, if he'd heard anything about her. Unfortunately, I forgot to give him the address of my parents' friends, where I'd be staying for the next ten days while my parents were in Europe. And since my folks had the mail held at the post office while they were away, I couldn't even find out if Julius had bothered to answer me.

Those whole ten days, my dreams about Belinda got stranger and stranger. When I was awake, I kept hearing the word "drowned" at the oddest times. Luckily, my parents' friends, the Farringtons, were really great. They didn't have any kids of their own, so they treated me pretty much like an adult. They took me shopping with them and let me pick out what I wanted to eat, so we brought home tons of stuff like potato chips and Cokes and candy and cookies and cake, mostly for me, along with a few items that were actually nutritious, mostly for them. Since they both worked and were gone all day, they gave me full run of the house, including refrigerator privileges, which meant I was supposed to help myself. I did.

The Farringtons lived way out in the middle of nowhere in what Nick would've called a suburb of a suburb of a dump, so there wasn't a whole lot to do except loaf around the house. By the end of the week I'd gained back all the weight I'd lost at camp and a little more besides. I hoped the scale was wrong, but I couldn't exactly lie to myself about it. Some of my shirt buttons looked as though they were ready to pop. I kept telling myself I'd do something about it. Soon. Tomorrow. Next week.

My parents loved Stockholm. They said the convention was super and the vacation even better. Dad brought home a couple of cans of Swedish meatballs. Made of reindeer meat. Interesting.

Next morning, Mom and I drove down for the mail. On the way home, I sorted through it. Mostly it was magazines and junk, but Julius hadn't failed me.

Dear Sam,

You are so lucky you can't believe it. The meals have gotten so repulsive, everybody says Langer must be recycling them from the used aluminum foil. Dallesandro's adding fifteen minutes a day to slimnastics. We're scheduled for another campout this weekend, but after the last one, nobody's worrying about missing it.

You left your calendar on the wall. Hope you don't mind if I keep it. If you do, tough nuts. Crossing off the days is my biggest pleasure. Except for getting on the scales. I have actually lost more than twenty-five pounds. My dad was really proud of me on visitors' day. I'm kind of proud of myself. I won the crown again last week. (I can just hear you saying, "Big stinking deal.")

You can rest easy about your sweetheart. They found her stuffing her face someplace, and they sent her home. Her parents looked like they might kill her.

Langer doesn't send his love. Sometimes at group sessions he uses you as an example of an idiot.

Write soon.

Your thinner cabinmate,
Julius

So Belinda was alive, unless her parents had pushed her off a cliff somewhere. I wanted to write her and find out how it all happened, but I didn't have her address. I could've written the camp and asked them for it, but I had the feeling Langer wouldn't even answer a letter from me, his second worst enemy. Especially when it concerned Belinda, Enemy Number One. He'd probably suspect we were planning to gang up on him somehow. I knew there must be some way to find Belinda, but I had no idea what it was.

I was still thinking about it when we got home, but I finally decided to take a look at the latest *Newsweek*. As usual, out fell a bunch of cards inviting me to subscribe even though we already did. I folded one into a paper airplane and was aiming it toward the wastebasket when I noticed that one of the other cards wasn't a subscription form at all. It was a regular postcard. Addressed to me. In an unmistakably flowery hand.

I flipped it over.

172

Dear Sam Zimmer,

If you are the Sam Zimmer of Cherry Hill, New Jersey, who was at a summer camp that shall remain nameless and then left on visitors' day, it is absolutely imperative that you get in touch with me at the address below. In case you haven't heard, I am alive and almost well.

If you aren't that Sam Zimmer, but you know the person who is, please pass this card along to him. Otherwise, this doesn't concern you. There are two Zimmers in the Cherry Hill phone book, and neither of them is named Sam, but kids' names aren't listed in phone books anyhow. And if you've never heard of Sam Zimmer, please don't bother me. I'm five years old, horribly ugly, and suffering from a number of hideous and extremely contagious diseases.

Sincerely yours,
Belinda Moss
29 Adams Lane
Reston, Virginia

22

Dear Belinda,
   I'm the Sam Zimmer you've been looking for. More so than ever. You were a pretty good prophet. Those Twinkies and chocolate bars and corn chips jumped right into my shopping cart the very first time I walked by.
   I was really worried about you ever since I left camp. I've been staying with my parents' friends, and I didn't find out anything about what happened to you until about ten minutes ago, when I got a letter from Julius. And your card. Now you have to write and tell me all about the Amazing Breakout.
   Enclosed is something I made with my own two hands and a little help. It's for you.

                                        Take care,
                                        Sam

   The post office didn't exactly set speed records. After two weeks went by, I began to worry that they might've lost my letter. After another week, I was sure of it. Then two days after that, a big half-torn envelope arrived.

Dear Sam,
   If you knew what a pain in the neck it was to find you! I begged and pleaded and told them it

174

was an emergency, but Cherry Hill directory assistance wouldn't give out any addresses over the phone, especially since I didn't know which Zimmer I wanted. So I had to find a library that had a Cherry Hill phone book, which meant I had to go all the way into D.C. The book they had was two years out of date, but it worked, so that makes me at least as good a detective as I am a thief and escape artist.

Anyway, once you told me you were leaving, I knew I'd have to break out. In case you didn't know it, you were my only real friend up there, and I knew I wouldn't be able to make it once you were gone. I mean, Marcie was okay, but if Langer had told her she could've lost weight by keeping her head underwater for an hour at a time without breathing, she'd've rushed to the lake to try it.

So I dug out my flashlight and sneaked down to the lake around three A.M. I know absolutely nothing about boats, but I figured the ones least likely to tip over and sink were those big old rowboats. So that's what I took. I plowed it into the pier a couple of times till I got the hang of the oars, but the rest was easy. There was enough of a moon to see by, and I rowed down the lake till I saw the first dock.

I had no idea where my cousin's camp was, except across the lake, but I knew it was called Camp Penobscot. But all the boats at that first dock had stencils on them that said Camp Something Else I Can't Remember. So I rowed on, past Camp Whatchamacallit and Camp Thingamajig—by this time I was getting pretty

175

tired of rowing—and finally I tied up at Penobscot.

I was wearing a Camp Penobscot T-shirt, which I'd had my cousin send me. It was small on me—no funny remarks, please—but it was protective coloration. I walked around till I found the mess hall, and then I waited in the woods until breakfast time.

I'll tell you, I know French toast when I smell it, and that was the first time I'd smelled it in nearly a month. It was driving me crazy, because I knew I wouldn't be able to have any. I mean, I had the T-shirt and everything, but counselors usually can count at least to ten, and if I just marched in and sat down at one of their tables, they might suspect something fishy. So I just stood around and starved, with that odor positively killing me, till breakfast was over and everybody was milling around. That's when I caught up with my cousin.

She gave me twelve dollars and twenty-three cents and an assortment of half-melted candy bars and pointed me down the road. After I finished off most of the candy, I started walking. I stopped in the woods just long enough to change into a plain, unmarked T-shirt.

Except for my aching feet, everything went okay. From what Marcie wrote me afterwards, the idea of an escape by boat was so daring nobody bothered to think of it for quite a while, so nobody was looking for me on this side of the lake. Anyway, I kept hiking up the trail, fortifying myself with chocolate, and finally I got to the main highway. Truly out in the middle of nowhere. Nothing but trees anywhere you looked. So I made a guess and headed in the

176

direction that seemed to lead the furthest from Camp Thin-na-Yet.

It was hot and sunny, and I walked along this highway for a mile or so, and then all of a sudden there in front of me was a mirage: a diner, the kind that looks like a shiny old-fashioned railroad car. Only it wasn't a mirage.

Now, I couldn't very well walk right by the place without having a Coke or something, and it was almost lunchtime anyhow, so I went in and ordered their $2.95 ham special. It was like something out of a movie. Half the people in there looked like truck drivers, and the other half looked like tourists, and there was me. I don't know exactly what I looked like, but I was the only person who wasn't attached to a car. Everybody gave me a suspicious look and the waitress asked me where I came from. I said I was just out hiking, and that seemed to satisfy her. She even smiled when she brought me my ham.

It wasn't the best I'd ever tasted, but God, it was wonderful right then. So when I finished it, I ordered a fried chicken dinner.

Gluttony does not pay. As the waitress was handing me the platter, a deputy sheriff came in and sat down at the counter. Didn't even notice me. A real sleuth. I kind of stared down at my breast and thigh in case he looked my way.

Then his old friend the waitress asked him what was up, and he said they were looking for a missing camper, and she asked him which camp, and he said Thin-na-Yet, and she said, oh, the *fat* kids' camp, and looked in my direction. The end.

Marcie sent me a clipping. The story made the

front page of the *Laconia Daily Star,* complete
with a picture of the deputy standing beside me.
My left side was cut off. Marcie said it was because it wouldn't fit. I could brain her.

Anyhow, I accomplished what I wanted,
namely a hasty departure from camp. Mom and
Dad were furious. There isn't even a remote pos-
sibility Langer will refund them even a dime,
considering how I ruined his visitors' day. All the
way home and for the past two weeks, my
mother has kept telling me how hopeless I am,
and Dad says he just doesn't know what to do
with me any more.

And they're sort of right. I have been stuffing
myself from the minute I left camp, and I'm
back up to my fighting weight. You know what? I
hate it.

Which is why my postcard said it was so urgent
I get in touch with you. I mean, we got our
freedom from camp, so why can't we get free of
our fat? I'm sick of my butt being the butt of
everybody's jokes, and I'll bet I'm not the only
one. So how would you feel about teaming up
with me in a big effort to reduce? We could both
read up on sensible ways to lose weight (no all-
carrot diets, please!), and we could provide each
other with mutual encouragement, and we could
write each other every week or so and report on
our progress. I don't mean we should be mar-
tinets about it like Langer and set iron-clad goals
or anything. Just put less in our stomachs and go
out and run around more.

I even found a book that has a set of exercises
you can do in ten minutes, which the guy admits
won't do a lot for you as far as losing weight's
concerned unless you shut your face once in a

while, but it's supposed to firm you up. The guy even talks about how much he himself hates doing exercises, which sounds like my kind of person. As soon as I finish reading it, I'll send it to you.

So here's my thought for the week, if you agree to this proposal (which of course you do, considering my awesome powers of persuasion): "More vegetables, less meat." Not exactly awe-inspring, I admit, but I'm new at this.

Write soon. If we work at it, maybe we won't be afraid to put on our gym suits this year.

Best,
Belinda

P.S. Thank you for the present. The expert employees of the United States Postal Service drop-kicked it from Cherry Hill to Reston, so I can't tell exactly what it used to be. A vase or pot of some kind, most likely. What it is now is a collection of shards that I put in a big glass bowl. The colors look super in the sunlight. Thanks again. *B.*

P.P.S. If you're lucky, the postal workers haven't ripped off what's enclosed for you. *B.*

They hadn't. It was a green and purple tie-dyed scarf . . . or wall hanging, I guessed. Truly beautiful.

This called for a celebration. I went downstairs, opened the freezer, and stuck a bunch of ice cubes in a glass. Then I opened the refrigerator, surveyed the pop supply, and took out a bottle of Coke. Then I thought about what Belinda had written and put it back again.

And took it out again and poured myself a glassful. You can't just go into something like this cold turkey.

179

23

I don't know how well we'll be able to keep it up now that school's starting, but Belinda and I have become regular correspondents. We're each down about five pounds from the weight we started with at the beginning of camp, which doesn't sound like much but is really pretty good considering how we both ballooned after we got home.

We wanted to be thin before school started, but every book we read showed us that it would be physiologically impossible. So we're on a program where we eat a little less and exercise a little more than we used to, and lose a steady couple pounds a week. At first it seemed like it would take us forever to get thin at this rate, but I worked it out on Dad's calculator, and it turns out that by Christmas our weights should be more or less normal for the first time in our lives. Hopefully less. We've vowed that if it actually happens, we'll get together somehow during Christmas vacation and show off.

Of course, that means avoiding a lot of holiday goodies between now and then, but we're trying hard. One thing we do is keep busy instead of eating. "Reach for a book instead of a sweet" is how Belinda puts it. The big trick is not to be obsessed with food, but not to be obsessed with losing weight, either. In other words, to behave like a normal human being. And so far, it's working. With the exercises, I'm even finding a muscle here and there. I think my big turning point was when Mom stuck a chocolate eclair under my nose just to tempt me. I refused it.

"You can't do this!" my taste buds shouted.

"You're ruining my reputation!" my stomach hollered.

"Pick on somebody your own size!" I answered. Then I slipped away from the table and shut my mouth just in time to keep the eclair from diving down my gullet.

I went out to the porch. An ice-cream truck was coming down the street, but I ignored it.

My fat self just couldn't take that kind of abuse. "I've had it with you for good!" it moaned at me, then waddled down the sidewalk toward the ice-cream truck.

I stayed put. But as the truck drove past, I caught a glimpse of somebody reflected in its side window. It was somebody standing on my porch. I didn't recognize him at first, but he looked kind of familiar. Suddenly I realized who he was: Zimmer, slimmer.

I'd never actually met him before. He seemed like somebody I really ought to get to know.

181

About the Author

A native of Pittsburgh, Stephen Manes studied at the University of Chicago and the University of Southern California and has written for motion pictures and television. His most recent books for young people are *The Boy Who Turned into a TV Set* and *Hooples on the Highway*. *Slim Down Camp* is his first for Clarion. Mr. Manes and his wife live in Riverdale, New York.